Also by Ellis Sharp

Novels

The Dump
Unbelievable Things
Walthamstow Central
Intolerable Tongues
To Wetumpka
Lamees Najim
The Orwell Girl
Neglected Writer
What Vronsky Did Next
Twenty-Twenty
Alice in Venice

Short Fiction

The Aleppo Button
Lenin's Trousers
(with Mac Daly) *Engels on Video*
To Wanstonia
Driving My Baby Back Home
Aria Fritta
Quin Again and other stories
Dead Iraqis: Selected Short Stories

Non-Fiction

Sharply Critical

ELLIS SHARP

FULL ENGLISH

Zoilus Press

A Zoilus Press paperback
First published in Great Britain by Zoilus Press in 2022

A CIP catalogue record for this book is available from the British
Library.

ISBN 9781838489847

Cover design by The Ever-Shifting Subject

Typeset by Electrograd

ZOILUS PRESS
York, England

The major parts of the clinical findings were brought together in my book, *The Function of the Orgasm*. I presented the manuscript, with a dedication, to Freud on May 6, 1926. His reaction on reading the title was not gratifying. He looked at the manuscript, hesitated for a moment, and said, as if disturbed, 'That thick?'

Wilhelm Reich

Ding-dong! Ding-dong! Come far? He wants to know, he really, really wants to know, Mr Smiley-Smiley, obsessive stretched suspicion-riddled curiosity married to a spurious good cheer, like a cop, the host, wants to know all about you, why are you here, what are you up to? he's worried you might smoke in the room, worried you might wet the bed, worried you might sneak a stinking takeaway curry into your room, wants to know what time you want breakfast, smiley-smiley, choose your slot, 7.30am? 7.40? 8am? sorted, yes, but, but now incredibly he produces the menu, you must choose now, how many sausages? the world's ending – it is – it's toast – toast! – time to endure a little longer though – time in which your B & B can be relied upon to make that diminishing more... sour – more sour than sweet – the toast – why IN HELL do they always bring you a rack of toast before anything else? – six slim browned identical tasteless rectangles from a sliced supermarket loaf in a ridiculous prissy Jane Austen silver rack – before even the small tumbler of watered-down orange juice – before the coffee – by the time you've eaten your cereal those slices are... cold as a corpse – after checking-in go out... a stroll along the seafront... cold... the dark pier... then back to Smiley-Smiley's... off to Bedfordshire... under the duvet at last... a glass of water, my tablets, special warning, this medicine may make you feel sleepy, dizzy and confused, this medicine may make you see or hear things that are not there, this medicine may give you blurred or double vision or have fits, if this happens do not operate machinery, do not take with alcohol, this might cause unpleasant side effects, such as feeling sick (nausea), being sick (vomiting) or very fast or uneven heartbeats (palpitations)... swallowed, gone... a splash of whiskey... several Diazepam 10MG, glorious... never see a sci-fi movie without them... half a dozen to get you going... doesn't always help... *Interstellar* was crap... but *The Matrix*... frabjous... and now the radio... no, not that... I destroyed my Radiohead collection... Tom Yorke just another little unprincipled rock shark... and Nick Cave... a sombre, creepy undertaker's assistant, his cold, hungry eyes... the eyes of a practitioner of necrophilia... a cool dry dark emptiness where a conscience should greenly flourish... rock scum... this is a true story, even the lies... last night in bed... I always read a few pages of a book before I turn off the light... tonight's the night for a Frenchman... as of this particular resonant and colourful and compelling dream-memory-night not yet as popular as he will become... *Phil generally had terrible problems ending his stories, mainly because he never knew what the real story was*... can't even remember the title now... slept well... except for that chasm in the centre... 2am, 3am... the past inescapable... good ol' Wilhelm... don't tell Dirk... all families contain at least one member who is deranged – in this happy family this person was the father – *Ding-dong!*... *Ding-dong!* a doorbell is ringing... thirteen years old... two o'clock in the afternoon... the year is – never you mind... someone is ringing the doorbell... thirteen years old... the south coast... England... Bungalow-Land... an estate of freshly built brick bungalows – street after street of them... bungalows everywhere... bungalows as far as the eye can see... built at the end of the nineteen-fifties on what was once farmland – a green plain in coastal Hampshire... a place where even today a few fields run down to the sea... today there are even more bungalows... the fields of wheat and cattle are long gone – today – at best – there are only two or three horses, in small fenced paddocks... the farm was called... but you don't need to know that... names don't always matter... this craving for names... closed down in 1956... I made that up... I don't know all the facts... the land sold to a developer... a new property... paint smell... one of the first bungalows to be built... Shangri-La... scene of a shocking murder... a husband strangled his wife... a domestic... nothing to do with this tale... afterwards he set fire to the bungalow... high drama... red fire engines... cops... reporters... solemnity... a scorched and blackened female corpse... years have passed... the estate when first built is full of sad white people... old people, mostly but... but a scattering of young couples, a scattering of the middle-aged, the lower-middle classes, they have standards, lots of them, but not as much money as they would like to have, very few households yet own a car, as for the Headmaster... Charles Block... he cycles to work at a big secondary school four miles away... as for Milly... Milly is a housewife, what would now be called a home-maker, her role in life is to look after her husband and her only child... Hollis... who wants to be called Hollis? a stupid name, although not as bad as Albert, Herbert, Toby, Ron or Eric... Milly is the first one up in the morning, making cups of tea, preparing breakfast, breakfast is porridge followed by fried eggs and bacon, later in the day she shops, tidies and cleans the house, bakes, cooks, sews, knits and washes up, once a week she goes to a Scrabble circle, which is held by a group of Bungalow-Land women, in the evenings she relaxes with a crime novel, she reads one a week, sometimes two, they are hardbacks from the local public library, they mostly have custard yellow dustjackets... she sits in her armchair... this family has designated armchairs... reading a yellow book... as soon as the murderer has been identified and truth and justice have triumphed she moves on to the next one, she has no particular favourite writers, she'll read any crime novel, by the end of her life she'll have read hundreds of them, thousands, the armchairs have floral patterns, over the years the roses and daisies fade... she grows old in her chair... one day she will die in it... but not for another 33 years... yes, all families contain at least one member who is deranged, in this family it is Charles... no television set because Charles believes television sets give you cancer... their rays shine across the room and channel tiny poisonous particles through the surface of your skin and before you know it your flesh and bones begin to rot... Charles is also opposed to the fluoridisation of water, this is just a trick of the chemical companies, to offload their liquid industrial waste... he is against many things, but it would not be fair to call him a negative man, he has interests, gardening occupies much of his spare time, he plants cabbages, potatoes and carrots... a large, long garden the width of the bungalow... it stretches back to a ditch and a fence, the other side of the fence is an old barn from what's left of the farm... it is not a quaint timbered barn with thatch but made of brick with a curving corrugated iron roof, it has windows, which are boarded up, in the ditch live rats, the barn provides a barrier to the world beyond, where there is an estate of large houses, posh people live in those houses, the Blocks are not posh... upwardly mobile... emergent working class infiltrating themselves into the lower bourgeoisie... in the long bungalow-wide garden Charles also grows runner beans... Hollis develops a lifetime's aversion to runner beans, he grows sick of the sight of them... dead language... strewth!... on his plate, nasty stringy things... not his first memorable food upset... before that – a good three years earlier – a severe mental trauma, a colleague of Charles's, invitation to dinner, plate was set down, you stare in bewilderment and horror... next to the roasted lamb steak and the two scoops of creamy mashed potato lies a scattering of bright yellow objects... yellow! the colour of vomit... just looking at them makes you feel ill... stomach throbs, churns, contracts, pulls... an acute nausea... like listening to Tony Blair... or the 'Today' programme... or watching corporate TV news... even Charles stares uneasily at these yellow monstrosities on his plate... small and round and sinister... defecated by Moroccan rabbits perhaps... makes you wonder... the host beams, proudly explains, these vegetables might resemble diseased peas or Moroccan rabbit excrement... in fact an exotic new vegetable... not easy to get hold of back then, quite expensive to buy, yes they came from abroad, imagine seeing a pineapple in eighteenth-century England... they are called... sweetcorn... Hollis feels ill, tells mother, must go instantly to the lavatory, a small cold room, Izal toilet paper, hard and crackly, lean over the bowl... choke and gurgle... nothing... no go... when back in the room Milly has removed the object of disgust from the plate and shovelled them on to her own... loves food... eats anything, copiously... Hollis is a sensitive boy, she brightly explains... he isn't used to surprises... perfectly true... he has his quirks and quiddities... still do... where sweetcorn is concerned always says No... no thank you... back home... better now... reading *Eagle*... this weekly comic is full of amazing wonders... sweet narrative! keeps us occupied, passes the time... Jack o'Lantern, PC 49, the story of Jesus, when the bad people come for Jesus they find him in the garden of Gethsemane, which is exactly the same colour as Roses Lime marmalade... best of all are the adventures of Dan Dare and Digby in outer space... the triceratops live on the planet Mekonta... Dan Dare's biggest enemy is The Mekon... he is evil, a bit Oriental in appearance, is mostly head, and floats in the air on a large dinner plate... Charles's commitment to growth included two apple trees, one of which died young and the other of which, to his surprise, bore a crop of plums, he also erected a wall of trellis, upon which he trained yellow roses to spread, the leaves became dappled with brown spots, the roses died, losing shape, crumbling around the lip of the flower... when he is not in the garden Charles reads books, his major interest is flying saucers, at meal times he explains that advanced extra-terrestrials are very worried about mankind's development of the atom bomb... the flying saucers are here to keep an eye on us and make sure that things do not get out of hand... some of the extra-terrestrials are so worried about the state of things that they have made contact, these ones are from Venus, they are tall and slim, with long wavy blond hair, they could easily be mistaken for Swedish tourists, the Venusians wear loose clothing and do not iron their trousers, there is a man in California called George Adamski and he has been lucky enough to become friends with some of the Venusians, they were kind enough to take him on a trip in a flying saucer, he saw the other side of the moon, which is not at all like the side you can see from earth, on the other side there are rivers and jungles and wild animals, he has written two amazing books about his alien contacts... a sharp memory of Adamski's famous photograph of a flying saucer... white curved landing gear... like three ping-pong balls attached to a saucepan lid... Charles was also very interested in the ghosts of Borley Rectory ('the most haunted house in England')... the Cottingley fairy photographs... the Abominable Snowman... the Loch Ness Monster... but one subject was never discussed... sex... *Ding-dong! Ding-dong!* now the rippling chimes die away... a leaden, heavy Bungalow-Land silence fills up the bungalow... hurry to the front door... be a good boy... open the front door... a woman is standing there holding a leather-bound folder... smartly dressed – buttoned coat – knee-length skirt – shiny black shoes – neat dark hair cut to just below her ears – bright red lipstick – hello, she says, smiling, are your mother or father in, no, they've gone away, they are visiting relatives... won't be back until the day after tomorrow... she beams... a warm, friendly smile.. she is like one of the nicer teachers at school... most of the teachers there are psychopaths and sociopaths... but there are one or two of the younger members of staff – all women – who resemble human beings... I am doing a survey, she says, I was going to ask them some questions but as they are away I shall ask you! what to say?... parents went away for three days... staying with Charles's brother Alfred... Alfred and his new wife... they did not anticipate that a strange woman would manifest her presence at their front door, may I come in? what to say? Hollis does not know what to say... this will only take a minute! her smile is warm and friendly... how old is she?... no idea... in retrospect... thinking about it... I see there's a flagpole in the garden... the wind lifts up the Union flag... upside down, as you'd expect from a B & B big brother... BB... Brexit... Boris... I think she was probably in her late thirties... just a guess... with the passing of the years the image of her is faded... probably dead by now... if not dead – withered... withered old woman with whiskers... thin silvery hair... dentures and a slight curvature of the spine... I suppose so, Hollis says, she steps forward into the hall, Hollis lead hers down the hallway to the living room... two o'clock in the afternoon... the curtains drawn... might seem odd that... it's because Hollis has homework to do... when he does his homework he likes to shut the world out... that includes daylight... prefers to draw the curtains and lay his homework out on a table... do it by lamplight... total concentration... a hard-working boy, takes his homework very seriously, father has warned on numerous occasions that those who do not excel at exams face a future of appalling poverty... deprivation... boys who do not pass their examinations often end up as bakers' boys, he says... those who slack may well end up doomed to spend the rest of their life delivering bread... that day – *Ding-dong! Ding-dong!* – it's history homework, an essay about the 1832 Reform Bill... remember very little about that topic... apart from pocket boroughs... an odd phrase... I should open the curtains, Hollis says, leading this strange woman into the living room, oh, don't bother on my account!... giggles... glances round... all alone then?... yes... smells nice, very nice... talcum powdery... perfumed... Hollis sees she is really, really nice... she doesn't ask why... why a thirteen-year-old boy is doing his essay like that... broad daylight... a curtained room with a lamp... Proust!... Let's sit on the sofa, shall we?... don't see why not... Hollis joins her on the sofa... she opens her folder... asks what newspapers Milly and Charles read... an easy one to answer... *The Daily Mail* from Monday to Saturday, on the seventh day *The Sunday Express*, magazines? Charles brings home magazines from school, foreign language ones, *Oggi* and *Paris Match*... these are very interesting... wonderful pictures and photographs... *Oggi* is very good on flying saucers, it has cut-away drawings of the inside of cigar-shaped mother ships, with flying saucers lined up on decks, this magazine also shows what the inside of flying saucers look like... whereas... *Paris Match* is good for huge black and white photographs... lots of photographs of people being killed... the aftermath of bomb attacks in Paris... a Soviet soldier shot down in Budapest... face contorted, body bent, photographed in the act of falling... abroad... violence... not like Hampshire... blood looks like oil in photographs... lots of it in *Paris Match*... the sweet inquisitor scowls, doesn't want to know about free magazines, wants to know what publications Charles and Milly buy and read, she's trying to build up a picture of their consumer habits... data... always a need for data... the motive to get them to buy more publications... I suppose... unless, unlikely, she is working for an organisation which really is surveying the reading habits of the lower bourgeoisie of a Hampshire housing estate... at the time Hollis understands nothing of this... a well brought-up lad... simply accept it... as far as H is concerned this woman is as – as authoritative as his science teacher – everyone in H's class likes the science teacher – he is young and called Henry – the whole school knows he is in love with the biology teacher, Miss Perkins – they have been seen together – holding hands in a park in Portsmouth – the kids are everywhere – they know what's what – the woman asks: what magazines does your mother read? – H doesn't know – she buys them from time to time – but she doesn't have a favourite one – H thinks they all have the word *woman* in the title – sometimes, when his parents are not around, H looks at them for the bra adverts – the sight of a woman in a bra makes H feel all tingly... can't really explain why... knows it is to do with sex... mysterious... his inquisitor sighs... H is not really as helpful as she might have hoped... then again... only a boy of thirteen... when not doing his homework H plays with his toys – a particular favourite is the Second World War, H plays this with his collection of toy soldiers, his Dinky toys, his Airfix aeroplanes, also half a dozen

14

German troops, who are grey, and the same number of British troops, who are green, also some Red Indians, who join both sides to even up the numbers, in this adaptation – this reconstruction – of the war drama, comma, the Germans have more planes but the British have more armoured vehicles, Britain always wins, not back until the day after tomorrow? no, and no sisters or brothers, no, you are quite alone? yes, H says, there's only me, not sure what these questions have to do with newspapers and magazines but Hollis has been raised as a polite child, when an adult asks H a question, H does his best to answer it, I need to use the lavatory, the woman says, she takes her coat off and puts it over the back of the sofa, H directs her, you go out of the room and then it's in the hallway, the first room on the right, after all these years – so many of them! – that is what H would particularly remember, her using the word *lavatory*, that is what it what it was called in those days, nowadays most normal people call it the toilet, apart from Americans who, let's face it, are rather strange, they call it 'the john', very odd, Americans are warm and friendly and voluble, which is what makes it all the more peculiar that they have difficulty in calling a toilet a toilet, H's inquisitor is taking an awfully long time in the toilet, what on earth is she up to? time passes and eventually H finds out, she returns to the curtained living room, she has removed most of her clothes and is holding them, a neatly folded bundle, in her cradled hands, she lays the clothes gently on the coffee table, the coffee table is an imitation antique, with bandy legs and a glass top, all she is wearing now is her suspender belt and her stockings, this is not some Victoria's Secret paraphernalia, this is simply what women wore back then, she holds a finger to her lips, commanding H to silence, H stares, paralysed, he has never seen a full-grown naked woman before – not even in a photograph, her breasts seem gigantic, her nipples are like a pair of big strange pale brown eyes – the sort aliens from a planet other than Venus might have, her jet-black curly pubic hair is an astonishing hairy wonder, H gawps, it is as if a Martian had just landed on the lawn and stepped in through the french windows, his life so far has not prepared him for this spectacular, bewildering, intoxicating, terrifying moment, while this unusual domestic drama is unfolding in the lounge, let the camera track delicately away, Hitchcock-style, and glide down the corridor to Hollis's bedroom, here, on the wall above his bedside table, hang a pair of African wildlife paintings, I say paintings but they are really prints, they are not remarkable works of art but slick populist daubs, heavy with the style of flashy realism occupying that bright sharp zone which exists on the borderland between photography and cartoons, one, 'Lioness, With Her Cubs', is a mawkish concoction involving three pairs of pleading dog-like eyes and a curled adult specimen projecting an anthropomorphic smirk of maternal satisfaction, the other print – pay attention, please, because this is the significant one – is titled 'Cougars, With Explorer', it's a simple effort displaying a watering hole guarded by a solitary palm tree set on a bleak arid yellowish plain with distant rocky hills, we are in Africa, probably, or, just possibly, the Middle East, in the foreground, on the left, four curled cougars gaze sleepily up at a fifth, which stands on all fours facing a man leaning on a stick on the far side of the blue pool, he is a youngish-looking white man with an extravagant drooping moustache, he is wearing knickerbockers and his other hand clutches a tin lantern, oddly, instead of the conventional explorer's pith helmet, he is wearing a keffiyeh held in place by a circlet of rope, slung over his shoulder is a satchel, his dark shadow fills half the pool, he is evidently a Victorian pioneer, a type, the kind of restless semi-aristocratic figure who wanders remote regions of the globe, locating the source of a great river, mixing with the natives, and reporting back to a select gathering in London on the strange habits of peculiarly clad foreigners, The Explorer, he leaves from the dock of the bay and returns to tell of the scarp of the Berg, he describes how a promontory of the high-veld juts out behind the peaks called the Cloud Mountains, he mentions with haughty authority and an even more rigidly sharp authoritative pronunciation *Ntabakaikonjwa*, which the natives know as *The Hill Which Is Not To Be Pointed At*, he has a picture of this hill, which he points at with a cane, unlike the first print, which unambiguously combines motherhood, parental protection and cuteness in a sweet tranquil sentimental syrup, the ingredients and atmosphere of this second one are altogether more ambiguous, are the cougars convivially welcoming the arrival of their visitor or are they hungrily eyeing him as their prospective supper? and why that lantern under the blazing mid-day sun? the artist, identified in the lower right corner by the enigmatic initials B. G. R., surely never came to anything, I imagine the English equivalent of Maynard Dixon of San Francisco, easel-painter, muralist, illustrator of the Hopalong Cassidy novels, and purveyor of sentimental scenes involving hazy desert vistas and noble solitary men in cowboy hats, Dixon ended up in a log cabin in Utah and likewise B. G. R. probably experienced some small commercial success, finally enjoying a peaceful retirement to a spick-and-span bungalow in Bognor Regis, be that as it may (and in this text it be, it may), I mention these pictorial trifles purely for the shining example they afford of the curiously razor-edged nature of coincidence, for looked at from the rusted and ruder perspective of today that second painting acquires fresh sense, its title resonates – but only with the passage of the years and only as language itself melts and resolidifies – you see – but you must know this – in time the meaning of words changes – it might take centuries; it might occur in just a few scattered years – semi-colons are in a parlous state – their condition seems to me perilous – they are like Top Shop and Debenhams in the time of the internet and the pandemic – to revert – to continue – for instance, in the age of *Hamlet* (last act, first scene, have fun finding the line yourself), the word 'politician' meant 'a sly rogue', a schemer, a manipulator, a practitioner of 'policy', that word meaning deception, misrepresentation, trickery, had they existed in Tudor times 'politician' is a word you would have applied to estate agents, journalists and investment advisers, today, of course, a politician is someone of dazzling probity, a selfless individual who is driven only by a passionate concern for the well-being of ordinary people and for what's best for the country, there are other examples of such deliquescence, in my own lifetime, to take the most obvious example, 'gay' has quite lost its core resonance of merry innocent vivacity, morphing luridly into the taxonomy of sexual identity, a more recent – a far more contemporary example – a more relevant one where this tale is concerned – we are close, restless reader, to the point of this pictorial digression – is the noun 'cougar', until quite recently a cougar was nothing more and nothing less than the animal portrayed in that dreadful daub above this fictititous boy's imaginary narrow bed, a cougar is a large wild cat with a plain pelt – it ranges from tawny to grey – it is found widely in the Americas, it looks like a tiger but without that striking unmistakeable striped colouration, but today, suddenly and mysteriously, and pertinently, acutely so, 'cougar' has acquired an extra meaning, it refers to a sexually predatory older woman, or – not all of our hero's personal cougars were predators – an older woman who engages in sexual relations with a significantly younger man, internet authorities require a gap of at least eight years in the copulating couple, although H's muddy experiences might indicate a somewhat greater span, the zoologists among you will have spotted a gross error in that print upon that bedroom wall, for cougars are not found in Africa or the Middle East, plainly a group of cougars could never have encountered our lonely explorer in this particular wilderness, no matter, the fact is that this print existed, a bluff dreamed-up to order by an artist who was plainly either an ignoramus or a tease, as a devout post-modernist I prefer the latter possibility, imagining a discontented frustrated individual keen to be revenged upon a commercial machine which had devoured his soul, I recall some years ago there was the shocking belated discovery on the tin of a popular brand of biscuits sold year after year with dense charming rural scenery in which, well disguised and very small, could be perceived, when you knew where to look, a tiny male with tiny bare buttocks atop a nude knees-bent tiny female with pin-head breasts, remarkably even a biscuit tin can possess a sub-text, human destiny – lawks, how sententious is this! – is always arbitrary, if H's father's education had not been strangely warped by his working-class background and by bereavement he would never have developed a fear of fluoridated water or an interest in extra-terrestrials, later, if H's tutor at university had been a wiser man, he would have foreseen the imminent arrival of Cultural Studies and persuaded Hollis to stick with the novels of Ian Fleming, instead Dr Dunlop urged H to develop his momentary infatuation with a dense, intense, contorted text where the adjectives hung like the sticky honeyed fruit of an overloaded, unpicked plum tree, arbitrary, yes, survey-woman, whom desire had made reckless, could never have known that she would chance this day upon a strapping thirteen-year-old alone in a curtained room, with his parents not returning for another two days, a rosy-cheeked virgin lad with smooth unwrinkled skin, now let the camera roll away from the bedroom with its risible prints of cougars and cubs to the pulsing, dripping predator in the lounge, commanded to silence Hollis says nothing as – she strips him of... his white cotton shirt, his grey trousers, his stained Marks and Spencer underpants – already those pants have – filled up with taut, automatic – male desire the tip of his – just peeping over the edge of the elasticated top – released from its straitjacket – points at the – sky – no – the ceiling – Cape Canaveral... strangely – taut... a rocket which has never yet soared... into the – gleaming – darkness which awaits it... the woman giggles – a surveyor – Kafka – removes H's black socks... close-up, a smell of talcum powder and perfume and a faint salty trickle – her armpits drip – watery – snake – slithers down across the ridged contours of – her rib-cage – her nose brushes against... H's chimney... drops down to sniff around its base – the grass – gorse bush – like a wet excited dog... takes hold of – his... hands, presses – presses them against her – nipples... H surprised – how hard – they feel... tiny pebbles... how... old are you? lucky thirteen... groans with... title of a Carly Simon album... all too much... stretches back – on the – carpet... swirls... drags – him on to – her... and – into – her... swallowed – up... left staring – her – contorted face... she's shut – her eyes – mouth – strangely twisted – as though by – intense pain – pubic hair – pressed against hers... feels – hard and wiry... jet black... adjectives being intensely adjectival – becoming bright verbs... words – melting... hands – pushing... pushing – him deeper... instinct – leads on to – do what must be – done... an accelerating – rising-falling – jabbing – blood-thumping – rhythm of – effort – the last chapter – the climax – arrives very quickly – just as – hers is ending – barely over before – she pushes Hollis away and begins hurriedly – dressing – put your clothes on, she says – you bad, bad boy – a harsh, cold voice – like an angry teacher – perhaps years later – you conclude – guilt – anger – the terrible risk – she had – taken – shame and ruin – lurked in the shadows like bad writing – like a TV drama – eyeing the possibilities – she – straightens H's collar – tugs his cardigan – into shape – you must never – never – speak of this to – anyone – she hisses – H recalls that exhibition of serpents under canvas on the quayside at Paimpol – Pierre Loti! Salvador Allende! – not to your parents, not to anyone, I won't, H says, you have a best friend? yes, Dirk, we go to school together, also, on Saturdays, we cycle to the library and borrow a book, then we buy some sweets and go back to his house to watch the afternoon wrestling on television, survey-woman's eyes narrow, there are still beads of perspiration upon her brow, they form two parallel lines, is this a genuine memory or simply fine writing? your readers want treats, a break, a sojourn with a cappuccino, a quick check to see if anyone has texted or emailed or voicemailed, as she leaned over H the biggest of these droplets fell silently and sank into his cardigan, leaving a tiny dark stain, ah! the simple pleasures of realism, in a realist text you are in no danger of encountering an extra-terrestrial, still less of being abducted by one, don't tell Dirk, she says, she gives H a very intense stare, you must *not* tell Dirk, she insists, he will only tell other boys, then our secret – *your* secret – will be out, H nods, solemnly, solemnity is of the age, Richard Dimbleby does it all the time, reverence, gravity, respect for the depraved Royal Family and the stinking corpse of the racist, Winston Churchill, the reason I say this, she says, her tongue sliding over lips, her wet tongue moving over her upper lip as if tasting it, the reason I say this is because, there is a handkerchief in her hand, she mops her glistening brow, because it is against the law to have sexual intercourse before you are sixteen years old, if anyone finds out you can be arrested, you will have to go before a judge, you will be locked up, she glares, you don't want that to happen, do you? you don't want to be locked up, do you? H is chilled at the thought, his inside feels like slush, the prospect of being locked up is terrible, a cold brick cell, with bars on a high window, he knows what it would be like, he has seen it in films at the Gaumont, promise you won't say a word, she says, her eyes are blazing, her rhetoric seems indebted to genre fiction, John Buchan? *Thunderball*? I promise, on the soul of your mother she says, on the soul of my mother, H repeats, leadenly, the formula doesn't mean much, frankly, the family are not Catholics, they are not anything, unless you count an interest in flying saucers and ghosts, the word 'soul' doesn't vibrate, it is more applicable to a fish, the woman smiles, a strange cold chilly genre smile, remember, she says, you must never, ever tell anyone about what has happened, I won't, I won't, and he doesn't, he doesn't tell anyone for fourteen years, and then, finally, he tells Honey, who is the only person he ever wanted to tell the truth to, survey-woman gazes slowly at the sofa and then around the room, checking that she has left no incriminating evidence, now there is nothing to convict her but the word of a thirteen-year-old boy, and juries in this era know that thirteen-year-old boys are pimply liars and fantasists, not that that ever happened, a trial, H kept his gob closed, his trap shut, his astounding experience a dark dark secret, survey-woman leaves, at the front door she formally thanks H for answering her questions about newspapers and magazines, now she looks just like she did when she rang the doorbell twenty minutes ago, remember, she says, *say* nothing, and don't tell Dirk, I won't, H whispers, closes the front door, it has a strip of frosted glass, through it the woman looks like a dark column of jagged shapes, the shapes shrink and jerk away and disappear, he runs to his parents' bedroom, it has a bay window, through the lace curtains he watches the woman go past the bungalow and up the street, she is walking very fast, half-way up the street a sin-black Morris Minor is parked, the woman puts her ignition key in the door and unlocks it, she gets in and drives away, the car goes round the bend in the road and goes out of sight, heading for the A6 perhaps, the afternoon street is deserted, the rows of bungalows are sunk in silence, H goes back to the living room and pulls back the curtains, outside, on the lawn, there are twenty or so starlings, they are pecking at the grass, looking for food, their plumage shimmers, as H tugs back the curtain they jerk away from the lawn and hurl themselves into the air, they swoop over the barn with the rusty corrugated iron roof and disappear, H goes into the kitchen and makes himself a glass of orange squash, he takes it back to the living room and continues reading about the 1832 Reform Bill, time passes, the waves break upon the shore, the knife twists in the heart, the key twists in the door, we must wait for the future to show, it's almost too dark to see, what after all is one night? everything, the knife twists in the heart, the key twists in the door, they are back, *Hollis! Coo-ee!* I am in here, mother, have you been a good boy? yes, mother, did you do your homework? yes, father, did anyone call while we were away? H's heart pitter-patters, a cold prison cell opens its door in his mind, no father he answers, wobbly voice, but his father doesn't seem to notice the wobbles, did you eat all the food I left you? yes, mother, father grins, winks, all that bacon? all those eggs? yes, father, I was quite hungry, he's a growing boy mother says proudly, they both smile, their son is a credit to their lusty copulation one hot July night, and how was Alfred? you may be wondering, Uncle Alf, remember him? H's father's brother, the one with a new wife, Alfred lives in Southampton, H's parents went there on the train, in some ways Hollis was disappointed not to go with them but Alfred lives in a terraced house with only two bedrooms, Hollis would not have minded bedding down on the living room floor but for some reason this was not an option, Alfred is H's favourite uncle, which isn't difficult as he is H's only uncle (Mother was an only child), he is about as unlike father as you could imagine, father doesn't smoke, drinks one small glass of cider per week, and is slim and fighting fit, father likes to do handstands on the beach, which Hollis finds deeply embarrassing, nobody else's father on the beach is upside down, so why is his? showing off, is the answer, father has a distinct streak of vanity, he thinks he is handsome, modest, wise and amusing, that first bit is true but the other three bits aren't, he is not wise, he is a dogmatic crank, who holds a lot of strange opinions, Hollis doesn't undererstand this at the time, of course, a child's way of seeing the world is shaped by home and family, how sententious this is, move on quickly, oh the sweet jerks and spasms of mental activity! the squirts and muddy gutters of consciousness! the wondrous elasticity of narrative unbound by a plot cooked up by the noxious conspirators of commercial publishing, enough, enough! back to Hollis and the days that are no more, the days when H used to believe aliens were watching from spaceships, television sent out dangerous rays and the water that came from our taps was in danger of being poisoned by chemical companies, nor is father half as witty as he thinks, the truth is he has a repertoire of stale jokes, many of them culled from the Morecambe and Wise show, he tells the same joke repeatedly, in a wooden way, the jokes are of the 'Why did the chicken cross the road?' sort (answer: 'To get to the other side!'), father has also perfected the trick of being the person who laughs the loudest at his jokes, his laughter strangely equine – a kind of triple neighing: *Nhay-Nhay-Nhay!* involving a strange, clenched convulsion of the tubes which connected his chest to his throat, Uncle Alfred is quite the opposite, he smokes sixty cigarettes a day, his fingers are yellow with nicotine, he coughs a lot, he reeks – reeks! – of tobacco, Hollis loves to watch him blow smoke rings, the way they rise and twist and finally dissolve, also Uncle Alfred drinks, the shelf in his kitchen is lined with bottles of stout, there are more by the fruit bowl in the living room, Alfred drinks several bottles when he come home from work, Whets the appetite, Hollis! he'd say, grinning, Alfred grinned a lot, he always seemed happy, unlike my father, who often seemed stressed and anxious with a subterranean anger, but then Alfred took life as it came, he did not mind clichés, whereas father wanted to hold it back or put it in a box and nail down the lid, father even had a volume of French verse, *Paroles*, it had a black and red cover, what happened to it I wonder, I never once saw him take it down from the shelf and look at it, Alfred had no truck with literature, he read the *Daily Mirror* and war books, he knew a lot about battles even though he'd never fought in one, Alfred used to be married to my aunty Edith, she was knocked down by a furniture lorry, Hollis doesn't really remember her all that well, she was thin and not a talker, she and Alfred never had children, but now Alfred has a new wife, Mary, they were married in a registry office and did not invite anyone, not even Hollis's parents, H has heard his parents talking about Mary, they don't like the sound of her, Alfred works for the Council and Mary is a typist, that's how they met, but she is only 25 whereas Alfred is 43, mother and father feel that is Not Right, what is my new Aunty Mary like? H asks, she is perfectly pleasant, father says, looking grim, an equivocal response, when will I meet her? oh I expect sometime soon mother chips in, and now we must get unpacked! the weeks and months passed, H did not meet Aunty Mary, the weeks and months passed and H did what he had been told to do, he told no one, he was a good boy, he did not tell his best friend, Dirk, that chump would never have understood, he didn't even understand when H tried to tell him about his first paroxysm, when he was eleven, he didn't know what this exquisite intense rush of pleasure was, he had never experienced it, when H tried to describe it to him he might just as well have tried to explain a volcanic eruption to a piglet, but then even H did not know the vocabulary, he did not know that exquisite word which combines the Latin word for a musical instrument which underlies the word – the (chuckle, wink, smiley face) very ambiguous word! – for a device consisting of pipes supplied with wind and sounded by keys, commonly found in churches and cathedrals, with that of the – so to speak – climax of phantasm, chasm, spasm, iconoclasm, protoplasm and (sweetest of all!) pleonasm, and owing something to a Greek word (which need not concern you, for having gone so far into this clotted text you have endured and struggled enough) as well as a French word signifying *swell with moisture*, it was several years, many years, before Hollis stumbled upon this word and, flushing, understood it, yes, how confusing and mysterious this era in his life was, grammar was the briar which blocked the pathway to expression, vocabulary was a dark vast forest on the future's edge, language itself was a matter of mist and ditches and sudden chasms, also up until the age of ten H was wholly ignorant of the naked female body, things might well have been different if he'd had a sister, but sadly – happily! – he was an only child, and sex education did not exist back then, at primary school there was the solitary excitement supplied by *National Geographic* magazine, the school library had a few copies of this sensational erotic publication, along with the other boys Hollis marvelled at the Africa features, which could be relied upon to include photographs in jungle settings where coal-black families lined up to have their picture taken by a friendly visiting American anthropologist, the women wore straw skirts and no clothes above the waist, how fascinating were those black breasts and nipples, some of those breasts were strangely shaped, with tips like arrows, reminiscent of the streamlined configuration of the rockets which whisked Dan Dare off to strange parts of the dark yet twinkling universe, that said mention should be made of mother's magazines, in the pages of which might be found images of busty women in stiff, plated corsets held in by straps, as it happened none of this had anything to do with Hollis's discovery of unusual pleasure, for that he had to thank athletics, odd really, physical education was certainly a physical education for Hollis, an introduction to athletics, if not the sort imagined in the school curriculum, remember reader that the English school tradition of compulsory physical education grew out of a nineteenth-century notion that to be physically fit was essential for a healthy mind, *Mens sana in corpore sano* – a healthy mind in a healthy body, balls of course, you only have to look at professional footballers to know that superb physical fitness and athletic ability is usually connected to an intellect the size of a pea, with all the conversational depths of a toddler, that said H is not going to knock a tradition which gave him his first introduction to – to cut a long story short – always smart – this is how it happened –

H passed the Eleven Plus exam, as it was called – eleven years old – ostensibly egalitarian but – basically designed to separate the working classes from the middle classes – the destiny of the working classes was to build bungalows – drive lorries – fill up your car's tank with petrol at filling stations – *BP Super Plus, Sir?* – come round and fix your wiring – electrical problem or – or – join the cops – whereas – whereas the destiny of the middle classes was to become – teachers – librarians – managers – bank clerks – working-class children failed the Eleven Plus – went to secondary moderns – middle-class children passed the Eleven Plus – went to grammar schools – G passed – went to a grammar school – however – his father – remember – deranged – didn't want – didn't want his lad going to – not the nearest grammar school – just three miles away – in the next town – Charles had a low regard for this school – full of young women teachers – most – possibly all – of a radical disposition – did not believe in hitting – children – Charles deplored such softness – the head teacher at a further away grammar better – much – a firm believer in corporal punishment – toughen the child – a good whack hurt no one – six o' the best! – hit slap whip punch – trousers down! pants down! look at those – impudent tender boy's buttocks! – they require bruising – empurpling – that impotent head deplored – softness just as – just as he deplored – unkempt hair! – unpolished shoes! – anything that did not conform to army rules – so off instead to Pudney Park – *Pudney* – a strange name – at first thought... the author! Hartwarp! – Johnny-in-the-cloud! – a terrific writer – no connection whatever – a Dickensian coincidence – pudding, pubis, knee, put-put-pud-pid-prude-pube-probe-pud-knee-pudney... Pudney Park County High School. Pudney was a village just behind the crown o' the south downs, it paralleled the coast in this part of Hampshire, south o' the downs lay the vast grey urban sprawl of Portsmouth, it had spread and solidified like sloppy quick-drying cement, north of it, beyond the green curving wall of the

South Downs, lay another community, the proles (in whom no hope at all lies) inhabited that ghastly concrete city which was out of sight but which was conveniently close and which one relied upon if one needed, say, a plumber, yes, here, in a tranquil Hampshire valley – a bourgeois Shangri-La – the downs sloped down to a lush zone of trees and quiet winding streets filled with quaint villages full of mock-Tudor villas built in the 1930s, three decades later these locations were infested by stockbrokers, bank managers, company directors and their progeny, sons were called Nigel, Cecil, Cyril, Dirk, Archy, Ronald, Charles or Richard, the daughters were all called Mary, Elizabeth, Anne, Hermione, Louise, Phoebe, Helen, Hilary, or Hannah, yes, here, set at the heart of a sluggish Tory paradise, stood Pudney Park County High School, the grounds extensive, with numerous playing fields, clusters of tall pines, a shrubbery, a rifle range, the nucleus of the school was a grand mansion built in the year that *Pride and Prejudice* was published, two modern wings since had been added, these framed the tennis courts, this establishment – such, such were the joys! – was run by a narrow-eyed brute, a silken Hitler, a twisted psycho named Cuthbert Edwin Lemon (yes, really), the Headmaster, nicknamed 'the old man', seemed old but probably only fifty, his peculiar surname was apt, he had a distinctly jaundiced complexion, also a thin, greasy moustache, The Old Man greatly admired Mussolini, a much misunderstood man, a dreadful end, Communist murderers!, he would often find an excuse to mention Il Duce at school assembly, the gist of his thrust was that Mussolini was a man who brought order to chaos, he had a particular commitment to punctuality, had he been on the staff of Pudney Park County High School, Il Duce would have especially deplored pupils who arrived late for school, C. E. Lemon's special interest was thrashing the buttocks of the adolescent male, yes nothing quite excited him so much as the sight of a half-bare lad, bending over, *Whack! Whack! Whack!* C.

E. Lemon became quite flushed by all the effort he put into the application of his cane, it had an ivory handle, as yellowed as the teeth and visage of its wielder, C. E. Lemon might have seemed odd were it not for the fact that almost the entire teaching staff of Pudney Park County High School were also sociopaths, psychopaths, perverts, fascists or religious nutters, in fact there were probably only two sane members of staff and they were both young women in their twenties, one we in the First Form called Pumpkin (because her surname was Miss Pumphrey), the other was nicknamed Perfumed Pat (because her name was Mrs Patricia Puttenham and she swayed across classrooms and down the school's long cold corridors amid an aroma of pungent flowery scent), neither woman lasted long at Pudney, Pumpkin was too radical for the Old Man, and Perfumed Pat was simply too nice, human beings like those two didn't belong in the school's staff room, and so it was that H endured his first year at his new school, he wore black shoes, navy blue socks, short grey trousers, a white cotton shirt, the tie and blazer of Pudney Park County High School, these last two items were navy blue, with thin gold diagonal stripes running down the tie and a golden coat of arms on the blazer, this coat of arms involved a unicorn, an elephant, three daggers and a small fort, all jostling for attention above a Latin motto: *paulatim ergo certe*, slowly, therefore surely, it was a mission statement which the teachers adored, they loitered in those long echoing stone corridors like cold-eyed rooks, repeatedly screeching 'no running!', anyway, twice a week every pupil had to attend Physical Education, in the summer this meant being out on the school playing fields, where boys chased a football and girls whacked each other with hockey sticks, boys liked to see the girls playing hockey or on their way to a hockey match, the girls had to wear short navy blue skirts exposing generous portions of plump pink thigh, but in the autumn and spring terms it was too cold outside so classes had to use the gym, P.E. classes were strictly segregated by gender, girls had The Bat (i.e. Miss Batley, a tall, muscular, wiry woman in her forties, with cropped hair and a hard, rectangular face), boys had Dog-Ends, I've no idea why Mr Murdstone ended up with a nickname which compared him to the discarded remains of a cigarette but Dog-Ends he was for all eternity especially now he has been embalmed like a mosquito in a pool of amber, to wit this book, for in black ink my memories still shine bright, Dog-Ends was fit and flexible but he was only five feet tall, his dwarfish condition was a constant irritant, he was known for his snarling aggressive demeanour and explosive temper, he was in the top three teaching staff for short fuses, number one was florid Mr Belcher (yes, really) the chemistry teacher, with a name like Belcher the chemistry teacher had never been felt to require a nickname, number two was tall ginger-haired freckled Welshie the woodwork teacher, number three was Dog-Ends, Belcher, Welshie and Dog-Ends exploded in rage at the tiniest misdemeanour, their furies were invariably disproportionate to the offence, all three men must surely have been suffering terribly from sexual frustration, their wives were (I imagine) equally grim, sour creatures who had never discovered Enjoyment, and so the joyous irradiating ecstatic energies that Dog-Ends, Belcher and Welshie were failing to discharge between the thighs of their glacial repressed tight scowling wives was instead left to ferment and bubble, quickly becoming a dangerous flammable mixture of vinegar and frothing acid which crystalised into razor-sharp shards of discontent (today, of course, angry frustrated people have Twitter), Dog-Ends was plainly compensating for his diminutive stature, by their second year at Pudney almost all boys were taller than him, it was therefore necessary for him to assert his authority through verbal violence, and the occasional slap or punch, in this era it was entirely legal to brutalise children by physically assaulting them, many of the teaching staff had served in the army in The War, the army did not tolerate softness, the army required total obedience to the command hierarchy and to orders, punishment was an essential part of Maintaining Standards, a part of Dog-Ends was still slogging towards Berlin in 1944, and there could be no doubt that his pupils were the sullen devious hostile Germans, or perhaps – now it is 1945 – the Hitler youth, crouched in a shallow trench with a grenade, these brutes in shorts must be beaten back, crushed, onwards to victory! as I was saying before the P.E. session began, with Dog-Ends screaming at the class to climb the bars, or do somersaults on the mat, or jump the horse, there was a five minute warm-up session, in these glorious three-hundred seconds we boys were permitted to do what we wanted, at any pace we chose, and so it was on a crisp September morning that H found himself entering the gym for the first time, what attracted him at once – ah, the strange alchemy of life and destiny! – were the ten ropes which dangled from the ceiling – ropes thicker than his eleven-years-old wrist, close-to the ropes smelled like well-oiled cricket bats, not as nice as Perfumed Pat, or even Hollis's rubber plimsolls (which H liked sniffing, when no one was around), but somehow pleasant, like the whiff of freshly baked bread, and so it was that H headed straight for the nearest rope and began to haul himself towards the ceiling, quite what instinct made him want to climb things he didn't know, perhaps it was his parents taking him to the cinema to see the film about Sir Edmund Hilary and how he got to the top of Mount Everest before any foreigners did, proudly planting the Union Jack on its snowy summit, or perhaps, as Charles was fond of remarking to his friends (with a hearty male laugh), in Hollis's previous incarnation he had been a monkey, yes, Charles was a passionate believer in reincarnation, he noted that even as a toddler Hollis had exhibited a propensity to clamber on to stools and kitchen chairs, and then the kitchen table, and, later, the roof of the garden shed, and, finally, the garage roof, sadly, the garage roof was made of nothing stronger than corrugated asbestos, which promptly snapped under his weight, and sent him plunging amid a shower of toxic particles into the darkness below, fortunately one aspect of his father's personality manifested itself in a reluctance to throw anything away, so Hollis fell on nothing worse than an old dusty abandoned mattress, and now, this misadventure and those early ascents all in the past, he is half-way up that gymnasium rope and this anecdote is about to reach a magical climax – but before we get there let it be remarked that in later years Charles Block changed his reincarnation hypothesis, whereas Hollis had once been a monkey he now decided that his son had been a Roman emperor, this was because as his teenage years passed he no longer had any interest in climbing trees or to the tops of buildings, no, it was not his life's destiny to become a mountaineer, or one of those fearless individuals who ascend to the very top of skyscrapers and photograph themselves hanging with one arm outstretched from the spiky aerial at the top, Hollis alas abandoned feats of manly heroism for sensual indulgence, he became a slugabed, to get out from between the sheets in the morning became an increasingly more difficult enterprise, he did not wish to be born, he preferred it in the womb, a nice warm place, where you were lulled by a gentle rocking motion, and the only disturbance was the constant rhythm of the ship's engine, and a voice, muffled as it echoed along many connecting corridors, singing 'Some Enchanted Evening', on schooldays he had no choice, he was forced out into harsh light, forced to smear his teeth with a minty concoction and then brush it off, forced to devour bacon and eggs while the night dissolved into another drear day, made to go down the drive and up the road to the bus stop, on the same interminable journey to an education involving a variety of dubious literary texts, *Farmer's Glory*, *Prester John*, I ask you, but not at weekends, on weekends Hollis lay in bed until eleven, on Sundays he did not emerge until five minutes before dinner, which was served up on the sabbath at one o'clock sharp, back at the gym Hollis is now getting closer and closer to the ceiling, but a strange thing has happened, his penis, which for ten long years has sagged limply between his thighs, has changed shape, it is no longer a soft, floppy rather ridiculous attachment, like having a tail at the front, now, strangely, unexpectedly, it has stiffened and transformed itself into a slightly curved rod, much resembling what modern supermarkets sell as 'junior bananas', he is aware of it, pressed against his navy blue athletics shorts, making the fabric stretch, yes oh yes, the coarse texture of the thick rope dragging against the upper inches of his peculiar appendage has nudged the dragon from its shell, a beast has hatched and woken, a delicate creature which has been slumbering through a long interminable winter suddenly has come alive, full of lusty appetite, a strange prickling sensation starts somewhere near the tip and without warning it begins, an abrupt explosion of pleasure – a stabbing, shuddering rush of sweetness unlike anything Hollis has ever never known before, even better than strawberry ice-cream, more succulent than spearmint chewing gum, more glorious than getting the ball into the net and winning the game for the Spartans, did I mention Hollis was a Spartan? C. E. Lemon, Mussolini-worshipper, resented Pudney's state school status, he longed for Pudney Park County High School to be no different to a public school, accordingly, upon being appointed headmaster, he decreed that all pupils should be obliged to join Houses, he chose them himself, there were three: Romans, Trojans and Spartans, you were not allowed to choose which one you would like to belong to, when you started at the school you were allocated a House, if you were Italian that was no guarantee you would become a Roman, not that dilemmas like that ever arose, because everyone in the school was English, apart from Irish boy, who was instantly nicknamed Paddy, and a solitary Scot, who, inevitably, was known to every other pupil as Jock, upon entering the school Hollis was designated a Spartan, Dirk was a Trojan, Spartans wore green athletics shirts for P.E., Dirk had to wear a red one, Romans wore blue, to return to that rope: Hollis hung there, shuddering like a Tudor martyr on his last gasp, his face a rictus of concentrated amazement and extreme ecstasy, sweetness rushed out from his loins along a river which some years later would make him vulnerable to the execrable prose of D. H. Lawrence, a flood making his whole body seem on fire with pleasure, a rush, a long, long shuddering, and then, eventually, finally, it was over, Hollis hung there a little longer, feeling his penis shrivel and flop back inside his underpants, Hollis had absolutely no idea what had occurred but he felt he must tell Dirk, but before he tells Dirk I must inform you of something which may surprise you, Hollis did not ejaculate, his boy's testicles were not yet mature enough to be manufacturing semen, he was dry as a bone, he was as empty as a cinema when the last show is over and the projector has been switched off, he was not yet ready to reproduce himself and become a father for the betterment of humanity, where sex was concerned, his penis was ahead of its two egg-shaped companions, at the time he did not appreciate the advantage of this strange biological anomaly, yes, no ejaculate, no evidence, no tell-tale slime on one's underpants, no grey accusing stains, *no mess*, Hollis slithered back to earth, flushed and still – *on top of the world, ma!* – gently throbbing, then small, psychopathic Dog-Ends began to scream spittle-flecked orders and the boys rushed to form themselves into a line in order to carry out a variety of futile acrobatic manoeuvres which did not compare with the one Hollis had just performed, did I mention (I don't think I did) that Hollis has extraordinarily strong arms? hanging regularly from a rope, some twenty feet in the air, did wonders for his muscular development, apart from the well known health benefits of serotonin, as it happened Hollis did not have the opportunity to tell Dirk about what had happened until milk-break, the sequence of futile endeavours orchestrated by Dog-Ends came to an end and the boys surged off to the changing room, after a shower, and after slipping back into school uniform, the class had to rush off to Chemistry, with bilious Belcher, the Chemistry laboratory always had the sour reek of chemicals, that figured, Belcher was half-man, half-acid, during this particular class Jock inadvertently switched off his Bunsen burner and Belcher, sensing insubordination, insolence and deliberate sabotage, exploded in a way we boys had become familiar with, his cheeks swelled and turned beetroot, his gigantic ears seemed to swivel forwards, like radar dishes, his right hand contracted into a fist, which he waved threateningly, he bellowed at Jock, he screamed that he was an idiot! a clumsy clown! no better than rancid porridge! a Glaswegian glob! a glue-eared glyptodont! (and so on), Jock was commanded to leave the laboratory and stand outside in the corridor – the conventional Pudsey punishment for the first level of classroom naughtiness, as glum-faced sad-eyed Jock crept like a beaten puppy from the room Belcher added that he would be required to remain after the school day was over and write one-hundred times *I must not turn off my Bunsen burner until Mr Belcher has told me to*, yes, sir, sobbed Jock, who was timid and clumsy and despite originating in Glasgow was not at all the embryonic Bolshevik that florid, paranoid Belcher suspected, luckily Hollis was a dab hand with a Bunsen burner, he always successfully ignited it and he had never once inadvertently turned the tap the wrong way, extinguishing it, yes Hollis was a lad who could be relied upon to keep his flame burning, fully erect, after Chemistry he finally had the chance to tell Dirk about his unusual experience, a nice feeling? Dirk said, indifferent to his friend's attempt to put into words the ecstasy he'd felt, yes, Hollis, like Julian of Norwich, was but a simple and uneducated creature struggling to articulate an extraordinary revelation and, as Julian frankly confides (in the old Penguin translation by

Clifton Wolters), before her great mystical experience, *my body was dead from the waist downwards*, how to articulate the ineffable? how best to express the noetic quality of an experience which brought Hollis from the chill periphery of life to what seemed like its radiant, shuddering core? even devout austere Julian struggled with that conundrum, in the end she wrote that *The good Lord showed that this book should be written differently from the first attempt*, an enduring truth, but the luxury of time and due reflection was not available to poor Hollis, he was hurled, nay hurtled, flushed, into the bright burning enigmatic heart of things, he did his best, yes, he said, he pointed, down there, that's rude, Dirk replied, there was nothing rude about it Hollis said hotly, I was climbing up the rope when it just sort of happened, my willy *changed shape*, and then I had *this very nice feeling*, but it was no use, he was wasting his breath, floppy Dirk simply had no idea what he was talking about, and now those of you who belong to diabolical professions like lawyers or literary critics will have noted carefully my statement that, at the point in my life when the woman doing the survey rang the doorbell, Hollis had never previously seen a full-grown naked woman, he had however seen the naked female form before his thirteenth birthday – and in the flesh – it just wasn't a woman, it was the girl next door, that's to say the girl next door when he was ten years old, her name was Hollisine, the coincidence of nomenclature made it seem as if their destiny, like that of Juliet and Romeo (*love* the Dire Straits song!) was written in the stars, when Hollis was eight his parents moved to a village in Huntingdonshire, it was promotion for his father, he ascended the celestial stairway from the rank of teacher to Deputy Headmaster, Hollis's parents bought – what else? – a new bungalow on a new estate at the edge of an old village, Chaucer Road was a cul de sac, which ended at a farmer's gate, beyond the gate lay an acre of ploughed field, Milly went mad with boredom being stuck in a bungalow at the edge of nowhere in a landscape that was as flat as a ping-pong table, here there were no hills, or rivers, or trees – just a vast Fenland emptiness which drifted off in all directions, ending in an out-of-focus mist, the adjacent fields were used for growing turnips, cabbages and carrots, there were no cattle or sheep, nothing moved in that vast desolation apart from the occasional distant big solitary dark bird, it might on a good day almost have been a town in North Ontario, most days were not good, they were grey, they made *ennui* seem like the old name for the parish, Baudelaire would have appreciated the extraordinary dullness, the ambiance, the howling nothingness, no wonder Oliver Cromwell, who once lived nearby, decided to overthrow the existing order and cut off the King's head, you would have done too after all those years of frustration and boredom, life in soporific Huntingdonshire left you yearning for some edgy action, years later I discovered that Samuel Pepys had once lived in this village, that also explained a lot about his subsequent activities in London, once you have lived in Fenland you have tasted eternity, and it's a very dull place indeed, get to it, you frisky dog, before the Big Sleep beckons, during Hollis's time in the village there was very little excitement, he had to make do with a toy paratrooper, who could be thrown up into the air and then his parachute opened and he drifted back to earth, Hollis was distraught when one day he threw his paratrooper into the air and his parachute opened up and then the wind scooped it and took it higher, higher, higher, his brave lonely soldier went shooting away across the farmer's furrowed field, a diminishing speck in an immense sky, until finally he was lost to view, Hollis never saw him again, his paratrooper was missing in action. Hollis mourned him for weeks, with the fierce piercing grief that only a child who has lost forever a favourite toy can know and feel, his father, keen to promote military values, bought Hollis a hand grenade to cheer him up, it unscrewed to allow the insertion of caps (tiny discs of gunpowder which were sold for use in toy revolvers – when you pulled the trigger the gunpower exploded with a CRACK!), it was only a toy grenade but sufficiently loaded with explosive it produced a satisfactory impact on the nervous system of dogs, cats and pensioners, but though for Hollis a hand grenade was quite enough to keep boredom at bay the same was not true of his mother, most of the time she lived in her husband's shadow, she was deferential to his oddities, a housewife in this society was not simply a homemaker, she also needed to be a skilled diplomat, but this time she put her foot down, after several months of village life she'd had enough, she wanted to live somewhere else, desperately, so Charles applied for a headship in Hampshire and, much to his surprise, was given the position, this was perhaps because the interview panel was made up of elderly males with strong right-wing opinions who welcomed the prospect of a headteacher who'd served in Her Majesty's Armed Forces, fought the Hun in the deserts of North Africa, and who had views identical to their own where discipline was concerned, a clip round the ears, a thump in the back, and the intermittent beating of a boy's buttocks with a wooden cane was just what was needed to combat the growing tide of insubordination and juvenile lawlessness inspired by skiffle bands and that gyrating American abomination known as Elvis Presley, yes the country was going to the dogs and the educational equivalent of a master of foxhounds was the kind of chap that was needed to lick these young puppies into shape, a spot of house-hunting in the area brought Hollis's father to the shining promise of Bungalow-Land, only two streets existed at that point but the developer had four more planned, bungalows galore! modern bungalows with a small drive, a garage, and a very tasteful wrought iron gate, streets which were named Barley Avenue, Paddock Crescent, Copperwheat Drive, but there was a snag, the bungalow was not yet built, so while the family waited for the builders to excavate trenches and put up walls

38

and slot in drains and waterpipes and electrical cables, they rented a house in Bland, and it was there, on a nondescript residential street which was as lively as a mausoleum, that I met the girl next door, my darling Hollisine, I no longer remember her face, but then her face was not the part of her anatomy that cast its spell, for weeks she was just the girl next door, she had a dolly and a soft toy dog, the dolly was called Mary and the dog was called Eric, as the weather warmed and I replayed the second world war on the lawn, Hollisine came round to observe the decisive battles of the conflict, she sat on the sidelines on the lawn, in the equivalent of neutral Switzerland, as the fierce battle raged between the Germans and the British, my centurion tank and armoured scout car blasted a path through the grey lead soldiery arrayed in a crescent formed of my Dinky toy racing car, caravan and fire engine, Hollisine, squatting on the grass with Mary on her lap and Eric at her side, appeared fascinated by the progress of the war, which moved slowly towards the inevitable victory of Great Britain, it was a period in my life when I was enthralled by toy soldiers, a golden time which would soon fade as my hands discovered other, more pleasurable activities, yes, the old enchanting thrill of miniature soldiery was briefly, momentarily, revived many decades later when, an ancient blotchy leaky wretch obliged to propel myself through the dead days with the aid of a stick, I found myself staring into the glass cabinets of the awesome collection of the sixth Marquess of Cholmondeley, this was in Norfolk, what spectacles! what epic clashes! what titanic tableaux! twenty-thousand little men with tiny weapons frozen in mid-battle across thirty-nine exquisite dioramas! once again the light cavalry charge at Salamanca! once again the Bengal Lancers advance up the Khyber Pass, ably assisted by a Mountain Battery of Howitzers, a weapon immortalised by Rudyard Kipling in his stirring poem (what a memorable title) 'The Screw-guns'! yes, linger like a whirring drone and gaze aslant at the farm of La Haye-Sainte, it is two o'clock in the afternoon on 18 June 1815 and we can witness the prelude to a number of strategic errors, unlike on my lawn, there, amid the green green grass, the winning side was always predestined to win, from time to time Hollisine's mother's face bobbed up behind the garden fence, checking to see that everything was alright, likewise I was aware of my mother, occasionally twitching the lace curtains to see that my play activities were proceeding without anything untoward occurring, it is now barely ten years since the publication of *Nineteen Eighty-Four* and the English middle class are already aware that Orwell has shamefully misrepresented the state of things, there is nothing at all wrong with total surveillance (it can be fun, too, watch *Sliver*), without it, how can one prevent one's daughter from becoming like that awful girl Julia, who is, let's face it, a slut, as for Winston Smith, no one called Smith can ever really be trusted to be entirely on board, besides, there was a lot to be said for the kind of firm leadership which Big Brother provided, that was what my father said, after reading an article about the book (which he had not read) in his *Telegraph*, I remember it coincided with him seeing a photograph of a Union Jack which had been run up to the top of a flagpole and displayed *upside down*, he was furious, he talked about it for days, he had not fought in The War so that after it the flag would be flown incorrectly, at times he wondered aloud if the wrong side had won, he did really, I must admit where that flag is concerned I have never really got the hang of those bars of colour, and if the thick one is supposed to be lower than the thin one, or the reverse, I not only don't notice, *I don't care*, in the third week of our brief childhood friendship – things moved much more slowly in those days – it happened, Hollisine was in the habit of popping round with Eric and Mary and mostly she just sat nearby, admiring my military prowess, like me, she was an only child, but this particular day was a scorching hot one, it was too hot to relive the Second World War on the grass, instead I decided to fly to the moon, my mother loaned me the wooden horse which she used to dry clothes on (foreigners cruelly deprived of English culture won't know what I'm talking about – let me explain that a horse is a folding frame which opens like a book), I opened it and tipped it on its side, to make a tent frame, mother loaned me a navy-blue blanket which I spread over the frame, and gave me an old towel to use as the base of my tent, although it served as a tent I decided it was a space craft, equipped with four digestive biscuits I crawled inside and prepared myself for action, just as I was about to achieve lift-off Hollisine's face appeared over the tip of my rocket, Can I join you? she whispered in her faintly husky voice, before I had to chance to reply, sullenly, I suppose so, she'd pushed her way in, Yum, yum, she remarked, spotting the three remaining biscuits, Can I have one? before I had the chance, sullenly, to remark: I suppose so, she snatched one up and crammed it into her mouth, her teeth crunched it up in seconds and down her gullet went one quarter of my extra-terrestrial supplies, her tongue emerged and passed to and fro across her lips, catching the crumbs which clung there like specks of dark sand, Yum, yum, she concluded, then said: What are you doing? I am going to the moon, I said, I gestured: This is my spaceship, would you like to come too? Yes please, she said, she came further into the tent and snuggled up beside me, This is *fun*, she said, she put Eric on the ground, Mary on her lap and her hand upon my knee, Ten, I replied, nine, eight, seven, six, pause, five, four, three, two, one, *Whoosh*, I continued, *Vroooom, Wheee*, up we go! Hollisine's hand slid an inch or so along my leg, I felt puzzled and nervous, *Whoo!* I said, *Wheee!* we wrenched free of the earth's gravity and cruised on through the sparkling wastes of space, the sunlight blazing down on the tent made the navy-blue blanket shine with pinpricks of light, it was terribly real apart from the persistent chirrups of a nearby bird, a distant impatient driver pressing down on his horn, the jangle of an ice-cream van playing Greensleeves, It's too hot, Hollisine said, removing her hand, I think we should take our clothes off, I wasn't at all sure about that, in fact I was rather shocked, in outer space it is surely best to keep your space suit on at all times, I said: Is that really necessary? She did not answer my question, I'll show you mine if you show me yours, Hollisine added, she was eleven and I was ten, her face bore the lascivious expression of an experienced older woman, she pointed at her crotch and then at mine, I had a muddy intuition of what she meant, already Hollisine was peeling off her skirt, exposing a pair of white knickers, Come on, she said, Get a move on, she pawed at my khaki shorts, by now she'd peeled off her cotton top and sat flat-chested beside me, I got a move on, by the time I'd peeled off my last scrap of clothing – my sensible Y-front underpants from Marks and Spencer – Hollisine was already nude, I gawped, I stared in amazement, I was flabbergasted, I was in a complete state of shock, I had never seen a naked female before, it was a moment of extraordinary enlightenment, you see I had lived for many years in a condition of complete ignorance of female anatomy, or to put it another way, up until that moment I had assumed that girls were like boys and that between their legs they possessed the same equipment: a floppy penis dangling alongside a small delicate sack of lumpy flesh, yet Hollisine didn't! instead of what I had she had nothing – nothing at all! – just a fine dark line which descended from her lower torso to between her legs, it looked like someone had drawn a perfectly straight line with a black crayon across her flawless skin, You can touch it if you want to, she said, her eyes were bold and merry, after that summer I never saw Hollisine again but I feel sure that in later life she had many, many lovers, she was that kind of girl, bold and adventurous and inquisitive, a risk-taker, a girl hungry for experience, gingerly I reached out and put the tip of my forefinger against her slit, I ran my finger down its length and to my horror it seemed to open slightly, as if about to swallow my little tremulous stalk of flesh, I pulled my finger back, as if it had touched boiling water, I was momentarily convulsed by fear, I felt as if that innocent-looking slit was capable of snapping shut and snipping off, sweat bubbled across my brow, in outer space all kinds of horrors await the questing astronaut, Now I want to looks at *yours*, Hollisine said, leaning over me with a hungry look on her face, she scrutinised my equipment, frowning slightly, there was a long silence during which I waited upon her judgement, finally she said, wrinkling her nose a little, It looks like a turkey, I knew exactly what she meant, the ones you saw hanging from silver hooks in the local butchers at Christmas, the pale pair of breasts with the long tubular neck and tiny head drooping down at their centre, a plucked, dead turkey does greatly resemble the male genitals in repose, Hollisine's hand swooped, she lifted my slumped penis in order better to fondle my balls, her fingers ran over them, exploring, What are they *for?* she wanted to know, scowling at that pair of pale testicles, they were the anaemic colour of an uncooked Walls sausage, frankly I hadn't a clue, they were just *there*, like my head or my kneecaps, I had never considered the various purposes of my body, assuming that they existed, eyebrows, toenails, the baroque bony porch of each ear, my dangling testicles – I accepted them without question, she moved on to my penis, I do not know whether it was nerves or simply that I was still underdeveloped but it failed to stir, it was putty in her hand, she played with it, as a kitten might with a length of string, she picked it up, then let it drop, and so there we were, convivially nude, inquisitive yet perplexed, explorers, and it was at that very moment that the asteroid hit my spaceship, catastrophe! *whoompf!* there was a sudden incandescence as the front part of my craft – a flap of blanket – was lifted away, sunlight gushed in, Are you in here, Hollisine? a loud harsh booming voice called, almost simultaneously a hideous space alien thrust its way inside, its head bobbed there, the sunlight creating a strange halo around it, inside this circular apparition there was a face – a very recognisable face but one which seemed strangely warped by powerful gravitational forces and perhaps the heat which melted my spacecraft as it plunged back towards earth, rocked by the appalling fire which boiled and seethed at re-entry to the green-blue planet's slender membrane of oxygen, it was Hollisine's mother, language seemed to die inside her throat, her eyes bulged as that agglomerated slush of anxiety, stupidity and suspicion which comprised her brain took in the stark horror that lay before her, the dazzling sunlight seemed to accentuate every aspect of the scene, sharpening the focus, there we sat, Hollisine and I, stark naked, while her left hand cupped my balls and her right hand held my detumescent penis in her sparkling sweat-beaded palm, a cry of absolute disbelief turned into a wail of disgust which increased in volume as it became a rising howl of horror and rage, a vast arm swooped forwards and wrenched Hollisine away from me, *Put your clothes on*, the vast mother alien hissed, *Now!* Yes, mummy, Hollisine coolly nodded, she seemed quite unperturbed by the interruption, her attitude combined modesty with the detachment of a scientist in an air-conditioned laboratory, the adjective *demure* might have been specially constructed for this moment, my companion on the moon mission, knickers back on, top back on, abruptly pointed an accusing finger at me, He made me do it, she said, He *told* me to take off my clothes, He said he wanted to show me his willy, it was all *his* idea, her eyes glittered with malice, a faint smile of triumph lingered on her childish lips, she was surely destined for politics and a seat in the Cabinet, I gawped, stunned to silence by her capacity for deceit, by the gross and simple magnitude of it, yes, Hollisine looked cute and innocent as a pixie, who for even a moment could doubt that filthy Hollis, his load of male lust lewdly displayed for all to see, was the foul and obvious instigator of these astonishing obscenities? I reach for

44

my underpants but Hollisine's mother snatches them away, Not so fast Hollis Block, she says in a cold controlling voice, her hand grabs my wrist in a grip which feels like iron marinated in a dungeon, *Mrs Block! Mrs Block! Mrs Block!* Hollisine's mother now resembles a long-playing record with an irreparable scratch, she hisses, she's cracked, she repeats herself, her mouth is open wide, her florid veined cheeks are stretched taut, her entire body is shaking with rage, indignation and nausea, *MRS BLOCK!* she requires a witness to my humiliation and a fellow judge to offer solidarity in the condemnation of my depravity, that morning I had a glass of milk with my breakfast, and then a glass of orange juice, and then, because it was a very hot day, a glass of water, my bladder suddenly feels in need of emptying, acutely so, nerves no doubt adding to the pressure, Please, I say, please I really really need to go, I need to do a wee-wee, Hollisine's mother snorts with disbelief, You aren't going *anywhere* until your mother has seen you, she snarls, her face is grey with emotion, *Please*, I sob, *MRS BLOCK!* her gaze is fixed on the back of the house, awaiting with keen anticipation my mother's appearance, and that is that and this is this, I can hold back no longer, did I mention that Hollisine's mother is wearing a floral frock? such is the velocity of the initial jet of cider-coloured urine that it soars as high as this frock, slashing and spattering and soaking it before it slackens and drops, it then moves down her leg as if deliberately, exquisitely aimed, finally it reaches her black leather pumps and burgundy socks, it gives them a good hosing down, drenching them in that pale, memorable, pungent shower, the grass around her shoes twinkles like flakes of gold, at first she is rendered mute with shock, then Hollisine's titters seem to galvanize her, *You beastly little – You disgusting –* words fail her, the word she is seeking is presumably 'boy' but she is choking for breath, she lets go of me and begins to clutch at her throat, her cheeks fill with colour and her eyes begin to bulge, one hand moves to her chest, which she claws at, she falls and lands face down on the lawn, she doesn't move, Hollisine has stopped grinning and snickering and is now silent, her face looks pale, liberated from her mother's iron grip I quickly whip on my clothes, the neighbourhood sounds quiet and tranquil, the distant whirr of a lawn mower, a group of faraway gulls, their raucous shrieks dulled by distance, the buzz of a plump zig-zagging bee, heading for the surging blossom-laden buddleia at the bottom of our perfumed garden, then Hollisine screams, it's an attention-grabbing scream, a shrill piercing concentrated needle of anguish, her mother appears deaf to it, she just lies there on the grass, not moving, I notice an earwig, with mysterious speed it's managed to mount this vast cloth-covered mountain, it is briskly making its way up Hollisine's mother's spine, and then my mother appears, she sees what's happened and turns white, after that everything is a blur, Hollisine and I are sent indoors and given a packet of cheese straws to occupy us while mother runs down the road to the neighbours who own a telephone, eventually there is the rattling tinny jingle of an ambulance and Hollisine's mother is lifted on to a stretcher and rushed off to hospital, when this is all over mother comes to join us, she tells Hollisine that her daddy will be along to collect her later, in the meantime we will all play a nice game of Monopoly, Don't want to, Hollisine says, hugging her dolly, I forget how the time passed that day, I remember her father arrived later and whispered to my mother, and then led Hollisine away, back next door, he looked tired and his eyes were red, Is she dead? I piped up, I wanted to know, I really really wanted to know, because death is a thrill, death is always exciting, death makes you feel grand to be alive and a bit superior to the deceased who has *passed on* while you are still in the great seaside resort of Life, watching the sparkling big wheel turn, knocking back a fruity pint, or a G & T with bitters, or a foaming flute, music is playing, the stars twinkle, the air is crisp and cool, the night is full of

46

sensual promise, but my mother just said: Hush now, don't be silly, as it happened – huge sorrow – there was no corpse, I felt deep sharp throbbing pangs of disappointment, high drama is always preferable to the pinched banality of the everyday quotidian, Hollisine's ma returned home a fortnight later, I was terrified of meeting her again, I felt sure she'd start shouting at me, she'd recall precisely what led up to her collapse, that liquid assault on the essence of her being, but – Hallelujah! – I was in luck, she'd changed, she was no longer Hollisine's grim mother who'd gripped my slender arm and shouted furious commandments at her daughter, no, when we at last came face to face, my miserable clenched burning heart swelling thickly with thunderous percussion and the iron clangs of a tolling ominous giant bell, the miracle occurred, she didn't seem to recognise me, now mysteriously she was no longer loud and bossy but silent and staring, her bellicosity had melted away, her vigorous, shouty, domineering personality seemed to have drained from her body, she'd had a stroke, a bad one, a bolt of lightning had blasted something away for good, her character was gone, she half-functioned as a human but she struggled to remember things, she plainly had no idea who I was or what had happened on the lawn in those minutes leading up to her collapse, I was neither a corrupter of innocence nor an impudent delinquent urinator, I was just a boy, Hollisine (bless her) must have kept quiet about our extra-terrestrial exploration, because no one ever said a word to me about it, perhaps (thinking about it half a century or more later) perhaps my frisky female friend felt guilty, she knew all too well that stripping off was entirely *her* idea and it was *that* which had set in motion the terrible sequence of events which had climaxed in a swaying anarchic jet of pale liquid gold and an explosion in her mother's head, soon after that encounter the builder informed my father that our bungalow was ready, we left the little settlement of Bland and set off back to the mainland, I never saw Hollisine again, except

47

in memory and my lewd and feverish imagination, in time her face faded but not what lay lower down her body, that first stark revelation of ultimate female biology has never left me, this was, then, quite a dramatic time in my life, at the tender age of ten I get my first sight of a naked girl and the chance to run my finger along her vagina, at the age of eleven I blunder ignorantly into my first orgasm, at the age of thirteen – novels are rarely as exciting in their plot developments as that, apart from the Biggles books and those of the Marquis de Sade, I regard it as a strange and poignant coincidence that during the week of my first orgasm I was reading *Biggles Learns to Fly*, its splendid chapter titles include 'Dirty Work', 'The Pup's First Flight', 'A Daring Stunt' and, remarkably, 'First Time Up!' P.E. was twice a week, which meant that throughout the autumn and winter of that year and the following spring I was enjoying two mystical experiences a week in the gym, and as Clifton Wolters wrote: Golden sentences there are in plenty, but in the process of isolating them a lot of very rich minerals are sieved away, note that well inattentive reader, having discovered an unspeakable joy (I never spoke of it again to Dirk or the other boys, who would have to wait a few more years before one by one they discovered that their tubes had more interesting uses than the disposal of liquid waste from their bladders) I couldn't wait for more, once on Tuesday afternoons and once on Friday mornings couldn't satisfy the pressure of my awoken raging desire, having learned that the route to ecstasy involved frottage I began a restless quest for alternatives to the erotic presence of a dangling gymnasium rope, my eyes, shining with lust, fell upon – I should explain that although the bungalow came with a garage, the Block family did not own a car, nobody on our street could afford one, apart from my friend Michael's father, who was a salesman, two years later our street salesman died in a crash on the main road to Chichester, after which Michael and his mother moved away, yes, death is everywhere, which is why

48

it is important to cram as many orgasms as possible into the time that you have, you simply never know when that creepy man in the black costume from the Ingmar Bergman movie will drop by for a game of chess and a quiet chat, the garage was cool as a larder, with brick walls and a corrugated asbestos roof, my father had put up shelves on the wall, together with some hooks, here he kept his nails, his screwdrivers, his fork, his spade, his trowel, riddler and rake, against the wall rested a pair of Wellington boots and a broom – a sturdy rod of wood with thick black bristles, beside them, the handle leaning against the brickwork, was a simple manual lawnmower which, when pushed, turned a spindle with curving blades, on Saturdays my parents walked into the next town to do some shopping and go to the library, they were usually gone for about two hours, returning on the number 31 bus, that particular Saturday I waited for twenty minutes, just in case they had forgotten something and came back unexpectedly, once I had decided it was safe for – but let's skip this chapter, night was torture too, I went to bed and read a comic or one of the adventures of Biggles but in no time at all that frisky friend – that greedy fiend! – between my thighs had woken up, sprung to attention, and was as demanding as a puppy, no, it could not be ignored, it was rock-hard and would not go away, like any gross and swollen tumour it required urgent ameliorative attention, however [section missing] I returned to earth as triumphant and satisfied as the first man on the moon, I put on my pyjamas and put off my torch, I slept the sleep of a rosy-cheeked lad with not a care in the world, things couldn't go on like this forever and they didn't, besides, every tale requires a twist or a shocking new development, does it not? if I tell you about [section missing] it is partly because my activities with [section missing] led to a sudden, wholly unexpected climax, but before reaching that explosive development let me toss into the stew of those days the remembrance of my favourite of all the books about Flight

Commander James Bigglesworth, namely *The Camels are Coming*, a text which is not about dromedaries or an American brand of cigarette but rather adventures involving a single-seater biplane fighter, the Sopwith Camel, it too has some marvellous chapter titles ('The Boob', say, and 'The White Fokker'), what's more Biggles was a teenager, just a few years older than me, but unlike me he was a clean-living fellow, who did not think about females or sex, his mind was on higher things, manly things, to do with combat and the ceaseless threat of The Hun, *Bigglesworth, popularly known as Biggles, a slight, fair-haired, good-looking lad still in his teens, but an acting Flight-Commander, was talking not of wine or women as novelists would have us believe, but of a new fusee spring for a Vickers gun which would speed it up another hundred rounds a minute,* yes, oh yes, Biggles twists like a snipe, when a Fokker sneaks up on him from behind he makes a lightning right-hand turn in his Camel and pours a stream of bullets through the Fokker's fuselage, the Boche machine lurches drunkenly and plunges from sight, a hit, a palpable hit! how little we know of other people, how little children know about their parents, how little mothers and fathers know about their children, how little lovers understand each other, if I squeeze out these marshmallow platitudes it is only because I have been looking at a box of old photographs, one of them shows little Hollis, here he is, a cute little feller dressed up as a Red Indian, surely an early sign of rebellious and anarchic tendencies at a time when every boy this age wanted to be either the Lone Ranger or a member of the Seventh Cavalry bravely riding out to kill the dark-skinned indigenous population, yes, even at that tender age Hollis identified with the oppressed natives and resisted the armed representatives of the genocidal settler state, this abominable photograph shows him in his prime, alas, also as a member of the I-Spy Club, a contradictory character our Hollis then, part insurgent, part Stalinist, a true voyeur ably assisted by the smothering sponsorship of the corporate media, a brat straight out of *Nineteen Eighty-Four*, the Parsons' boy!, here he is on the Bungalow-Land lawn, adopting a posture which makes him wonder in later years if perhaps he should not have become a yoga instructor, how proudly, cross-legged, he displays his collection of I-Spy Books, together with the Certificates which he has received from Big Chief I-Spy, who lives at the *Daily Mail* head office, if I am not much mistaken the blanket draped around the upper half of his body is the very same navy-blue sheet that formed the fuselage of his space rocket to the moon, yes, he may look a little smug and self-satisfied and, magnified and scrutinised, bearing a strong resemblance to a young Aleister Crowley, even, perhaps, the actor playing Casanova in the enticing third episode of Francesco da Mosto's delightful Venice documentary, although inside surely more like John Gillespie Magee, having done a hundred things, or the dying replicant in *Blade Runner*, he's seen things – known things – which Dirk and his other male friends wouldn't believe, later, decades will pass, Hollis will forget a great deal, but – the big BUT – he will remember one particular day quite vividly, it was a Saturday, not long after that photograph was taken, the sun was shining, making the yellow drawn curtains in his bedroom glow with good health, like a spotless banana, his parents had gone out shopping and would be gone for a good two to three hours, he waited half an hour and then sprang into action, they had left him in bed, he quickly slipped off his striped jim-jams and – and – and – the mechanism need not concern the reader, who is surely, please, so much more than herself a deplorable sweating voyeur with a tongue wetly roaming around the succulent edges of a dripping mouth – this was when it happened. O.M.G. (as youngsters say nowadays), rush after rush of acute spreading fiery sweetness, as usual, but to his astonishment and horror something else also happened – an event for which our lamentable and bewildered protagonist was utterly unprepared, just as was his fellow innocent on that memorable eighth day of May, 1373, when she, as the reader will surely know – will surely not require reminding – witnessed the copious shedding of blood, a continual bleeding, great drops of it, rolling down from the garland-like beads, apparently from broken veins, a rich brownish red colour – thick, thick, thick – and each bead spreading out, oozing, becoming bright red, the colour of the berries on an English yew, moving on to touch His eyebrows, blood astonishingly fresh and lively, so much blood, falling so thickly, thickly, thickly it was impossible to count them, reminding our witness in turn of beads, of herring scales and of raindrops, a perception – a richly figurative one, as in the best they are – obtained, surely, from the horizontal, aided by, one might surmise, a wandering palm, perhaps, perhaps simply a forefinger, or a forefinger and its taller neighbour, we'll never really know, transcendence is ineffable, if so a marked contrast to Hollis, whose posture, an unusual and idiosyncratic one involving a pinewood wardbrobe, was – we get to the crux of this matter – predominantly vertical at the moment of amazement, an extraordinary moment – it came out of the blue – here it comes – a sudden bolt of slime, abruptly jetted from the gaping mouth of a goldfish face attached to the hard, swollen ardour of a pike, it shot, this astonishing substance, this unexpected mucus, upward, unfolding itself, just missing our protagonist's nose, after which it continued its trajectory, slapping itself at last against the bedroom ceiling, a considerable shock, a moment which was quite simply the prologue to a greater drama as quivering shivering shuddering Hollis had barely time to register this blur of fluid before more came pumping out, each throb of ecstasy hurtling yet more bolts, soaring like a bird in a Gerard Manley Hopkins poem, on the trail of the shining Lord, soaring, up, up, up, and then folding and falling, as if brought down by a florid prince with a double-barrelled instrument of murder, the next moment, as though Hollis was out in the wilds on a stroll with the legendary naked rambler, except that he had lost sight of his mentor and was now entirely alone – the thought of King Lear crossed his mind – and stood there, shivering, splattered by the first wave of inclement weather, Hollis's chin, as yet unscarred by Life and an oaf with a flashing silver blade, felt the liquid smacks of projectiles returning from a voyage into the unknown, propelled by gravity's powerful invisible pressure, simply the stark continuance of a drama which more and more comes to rival that of an old man on a storm-swept heath, yes, more and more arrived, how it came tumbling down, falling across his chest and stomach, the final few drops landing almost at the launch site, in a nest of a boy's soft velvety pubic hair, poor Hollis, poor bewildered lad, he was perplexed and aghast at this wholly unexpected development, what a hideous mess! this glistening muck was everywhere, the dark triangle of curly hair above his genitals was threaded with it, as if it was Christmas and silver ribbons had been hung there, a preposterous metaphor, surely, for truly it looked like nothing so much as snot, repellent as any personage whose unattended nose drips a thick gleaming trail that cries out to be wiped off and dealt with, yes, it dripped from his chin as though he was Winnie-the-Pooh and had been at the honey pot again, it was smeared across his chest, it clung tenaciously like glue to the little line of hair which ran in a vertical line down his stomach, some of it had got on to the wardrobe, the soft sensuous fresh pine-smelling corner's edge glittered with it, like a snail's trail on stone on a sunlit winter morn, worst of all was that startlingly substantial blob on the ceiling which hung there like a grey accusing eye, swollen with reproach, and even as Hollis watched it began marvellously to change shape, yes, shifting its contours it adopted the outline of a small pear, a mysterious crop brought to life by a ceiling which had consorted with some sweating fertile darkness in the unseen loft above it, a kind of jelly, a lively little mould, some sort of monstrous animated fungus, yes, truly

53

it seemed to possess a life of its own, making Hollis wonder anew about the enigma of Life of which he knew so little, and in that terrifying existential moment he wondered if in thrall to his addiction, his secret life, his lonesome voyage into the unknown, had he somehow blundered and fallen away from all that keeps humanity on an even keel, had he – *the horror, the horror* – given birth to something small and monstrous, like an astronaut on a far distant planet who has had illicit contact with an alien life form, question mark, exclamation, yes, there was no escaping the evidence of his guilt, it lay all around him, like that of a murderer who is found in a splattered room, the carpets drenched, holding a wet scarlet knife above a savagely mutilated corpse – Hollis let go of his weapon – yes – *I will show you fear in a handful of slime* – his gaze returned to the ceiling – it was a moment every bit as dreadful as that scene in *Tess of the D'Urbervilles* – the seconds pass – the electric clock in the kitchen softly notes the slow passage of the twentieth century – and now it happens – obedient to Newton's law of universal gravitation – the miniature pear wobbles – it stretches itself – it slips from the ceiling's surly bonds – it falls – it hits the rug below – a stain the size of a halfpenny – that's it – stasis – it's all over now – beyond the lace curtains a milk float passes – the clatter of empty pint bottles bouncing in their crates – other bottles brimful of white liquid – the cream at the spout – the shapes of the bottles – cool and fresh – just waiting to be emptied – yes, that was that – several bungalows away a dog started barking – Hollis stood in that quiet room knowing for the first time what it must feel like to be a killer in those first few terrible minutes after the crime has been committed – the thud of guilt – the evidence everywhere – time was passing – was that a vehicle slowing to a halt outside? – it was like Macbeth and Mrs Macbeth – a sticky situation – water is needed – go fetch it! – your heart is like thunder – you run into the bathroom – soap, water, a creamy froth! – apply yourself – a brisk towel-rub afterwards – hygienic once again – innocent as a cute-eyed kitten – back to the bedroom – clothes on – next the kitchen – rummage in the cupboard under the sink – find a suitable rag – back to the bedroom – give the wardrobe a wipe – the easy bit – next the rug – oh Lord! – soap and water leaves a dark stain bigger than before – press a towel against the sodden fibres, dry them, do your best – lastly that mark on the ceiling – though the pear has fallen from the tree a grey smear remains – a gentle wipe should do the trick – no, yet more horror! – some of the white paint has come off – a tell-tale mark bigger than a half-crown – leave it at that – hope no one notices – nobody normally looks at ceilings, do they? – leave it, depart, off to the kitchen for a nourishing bowl of Kellogg's Cornflakes – but do not think poor Hollis was now at peace, on the contrary, his mind was greatly troubled, he simply didn't understand what had occurred, was he sick? was his body in revolt? he just didn't know, he was lost at sea, he was a stranger in a strange land, somehow he got through the rest of that day, the parentals returned with their shopping, lunch was prepared and eaten, in the afternoon he played with his Dinky toys, in the evening he read several chapters of *Biggles and the Cruise of the Condor*, his mother bustled in and out of his bedroom a few times but, like a blundering policeman in one of her yellow-jacketed crime thrillers, she failed to notice anything amiss, meanwhile his father threw down his poltergeist book saying that Sacheverell Sitwell was a fool, apparently Sitwell didn't believe in the paranormal, he thought poltergeist activity was caused by mentally disturbed teenagers, a sexual dimension might be deemed to be present, the man is an idiot, father said, he scowled, *Teenagers!* he spat, he snorted like a pig, then glared in Hollis's direction, as if somehow he was to blame, technically, however, he was only eleven years old and therefore not yet a teenager, but then, Charles hissed, beginning to smile, what can you expect from a man whose first name is Sacheverell, a sissy name, a bit *French*, when you came to think about it, not manly, not manly at all, Charles was speaking as usual to himself, mother had returned to the living room and was engrossed in *The Case of the One-Eyed Witness*, father's monologue washed over her as the waves roll over a rock, Hollis was trying to concentrate on his Biggles book and not think about that strange sticky fluid, at ten he went to bed, he lay there in torment, was he ill? diseased? had his journeys into the transcendent produced a dark reaction in his body? there was only one way to find out, he waited until the usual sequence of night-time events had played out, involving flushed lavatories and that decisive pulling of the light cord in the adjacent bedroom, he lay there for twenty minutes waiting for his father to begin snoring, another ten minutes, and then H applied himself to the great question of the present time, on this occasion – smart lad! – he took the precaution of using a handkerchief, wrapping it gently around the source of potential difficulty, a wise move as it turned out, he quickly learned that he would have to cope with his new affliction as best he could, from now on he was doomed to experience an inescapable side effect, the dry phase of his life was over, the future could only ever be a liquid one, Life could only become more challenging in a world where soft tissue had yet to be invented and where language continued to outwit him, for poor Hollis could not put a name to the grey dense soup which flooded his delights, there was a word which he would not discover for many more years, proving – if I may make a philosophical point – that existence precedes essence, although there were glimmerings, oh yes there were glimmerings, one somehow got to hear of a dangerously risqué word whispered by snickering older boys at Pudney Park County High School, and that word was *spunk*, yes, the older boys sniggered and winked, some even intimated that they had donated some to the voluptuous young French mistress, Mademoiselle Roubaud, although everyone knew they hadn't, or thought so, until one day Miss Roubaud abruptly left, and there was talk of a scandal involving a boy named Pritchard, yet the mechanics of such murky matters were still as baffling to Hollis – and about as comprehensible – as an electrical generator wrapped in cardboard and marooned in fog, yes, it would take time for the fog to lift and for the packaging to be removed, and so the months soupily passed until one grey day Hollis's father thrust a green booklet at him, Read this, he said, You do not need to return it, keep it in your room, then, flushing a little, he hurried away, *The Golden Pathway to a Healthy Body*, Hollis opened it, a little perplexed by this gift, no author was named, it was non-fiction, which explained it, its authority was assumed, the message, repeated with thudding regularity, was the importance of *A Healthy Body*, this could be accomplished with Regular Baths, Attention to the Toenails and Fingernails, and Frequent Exercise, there were as many words beginning with capital letters as any stretch of German prose, well let it be said that Hollis was certainly a lad keen on Frequent Exercise, his arms seemed to grow stronger with every month that passed, his testicles glowed like tomatoes in a sunlit greenhouse, they hung like ripe plums, Hollis didn't know it but he was in his biological prime, he could have fathered a dozen Hollises a week had the appropriate incubation receptacles been available, Make Sure You Can Touch Your Toes, a boy who cannot touch his toes is out of shape, he should seek advice from his physical exercise instructor (the booklet advised), and don't forget those Regular Baths! so far so banal – but then the booklet moved on to sex, or rather to a baffling section devoted to two topics, the first was 'self-pollution', written in euphemisms about Unhealthy Instincts, these pernicious instincts led to tiredness and loss of concentration, one would not get on at school if one polluted oneself, plus there was an even more baffling section, it was devoted to 'women of the night' and 'women of loose morals', deeply puzzling categories of female, what women of the night, question mark, for Hollis had never noticed any strange women at night in Bungalow-Land and even if there were any of these lethal loiterers – was it possible the booklet meant vampires?– they certainly didn't come into the Block's garden (whether or not the same held true for the Finzi-Continis across the street was another matter), the booklet explained that women of the night were there to satisfy Base Appetites, Hollis wondered what that meant, chips with strawberry jam? fried eggs and chocolate ice-cream? even worse, they gave men diseases, these nocturnal females, if you had anything to do with them you would fall sick and might well die, you would almost certainly become very ill, your body would become covered in scabs and sores, little drill-shaped creatures would worm their way through your insides, eating you up, you might well lose parts of your body that you would not wish to lose, your nose, for example, Women of Loose Morals were no better, they threatened the Temple of the Human Body and the Sanctity of Marriage, they made everybody unhappy, this last section climaxed (so to speak) with a poem by Arthur Hugh Clough, 'Say not the struggle nought availeth', like so much of this booklet Hollis didn't understand it at all: *If hopes were dupes, fears may be liars; / It may be, in yon smoke concealed, / Your comrades chase e'en now the fliers, / And, but for you, possess the field*, that's as clear as mud (as uncle used to say), Hollis liked the last line, though, that definitely had something, *But westward, look, the land is bright*, beside this poem a curly-haired lad in shorts stared at some billowing cumulonimbus, from behind which the sun sent slender cone-shaped rays which resembled the spokes of a bicycle wheel, an upbeat ending, the lad had evidently managed to dodge those mysterious women of the night and the ones with loose morals and our hero was on his way to where the sunshine is, judging by the picture this place was Switzerland, I don't think anybody much reads Arthur Hugh Clough any more, do they? although I expect if I Googled it I'd discover there was an

Arthur Hugh Clough Society, the internet is invaluable for bringing together those of a like-minded disposition, be it an interest in Latvian flying saucers or minor Victorian poets, so it goes, Hollis put the booklet down, it took some time before he realised what *unhealthy instincts* involved, and though he decided to combat them like the lad in the sunshine the point came – usually after about three days – when he could hold back no longer, no matter what the risk, premature baldness, fatigue, loss of concentration on his homework, failing eyesight, blindness, yes, yes, oh yes, something else, in those days a boy had to use his imagination, when a boy mounted a pine wardrobe he was not embracing furniture with a faint hint of varnish but the lithe limbs of Mademoiselle Roubaud, Do eet to me, she whispered in that enticing accent of hers, and he duly did, although quite what it was he was doing was always a little cloudy, so very different to today when a boy Hollis's age would be found hunched over a device, watching a gleaming busy busty transfixed porn star absorb more arrows than Edmund the Martyr, and now society and culture begin to change, syrup starts to congeal and then evaporate, Perry Como's sales decline, Alma Cogan's Tennessee Waltz fails to wow, the wireless begins to gestate rock groups, Charles Block scorns pop music (he senses that Communist Russia is behind it, somehow), he deplores men with lacy shirts and long hair, long hair on men threatens his notion of masculinity, which involves a short back and sides, handstands, a well-adjusted tie and black shoes which gleam with polish, as for lacy shirts, they are like a woman's blouse, no man who is not some kind of pervert would ever wear a shirt like that, The Rolling Stones in particular disgust him, that Jagger fellow ought to be put in the army, that would sort out his nonsense, Hollis's father finds guitars disturbing, Hollis asked his mother if he could have one for Christmas but after consulting father the response was No, the reason given was that a guitar would distract him from his homework (just like self-pollution!), he might be tempted to twiddle nylon strings instead of solving complex mathematical puzzles, strumming threatened the integrity of education, he must not be tempted by chords when instead he should be working out how long it takes a water-pipe three inches in circumference to fill a bath six feet long by two feet wide if it takes 55 seconds to fill one inch of that bath, but before the jury's verdict was announced he overheard them whispering, father was saying that a guitar bore a disturbing resemblance to a woman's body, the thought of his son cradling the wooden simulacrum of a small woman's body and plucking at what was effectively her navel was, he decisively concluded, *unwholesome*, no, there must be absolutely no self-produced music, it was like – well, never mind what it was like – but in fact *The Golden Pathway to a Healthy Body* was wrong about the perils of pollution, pollution did not induce lassitude and loss of concentration, on the contrary, Hollis adored reading, facts, history and novels, his mind – his curiosity – was as acute as his appetites, yes, even the school syllabus could at times be enthralling, one of the set texts in that year which Nature had decided he was fit for fatherhood was *Prester John* by John Buchan – and what a cracker this book turned out to be! in later life he bought all Buchan's novels, including this one, yes, unlike many popular writers his fiction has never gone out of print, his prose remains as clear and lucid and fresh as when his books were first published, and what plots! in those days the blurbs gave away the entire plot, *Prester John tells how young Scotsman David Crawfurd* (sic) *thwarts a black uprising in South Africa, John Laputa, a black fanatic, is trying to revive the empire of Prester John, a legendary African king, stirring up trouble among the Kaffir tribes, Laputa is believed to be obtaining money to purchase arms by collaborating with a gang of illicit diamond dealers, all he needs to crown his power is possession of a mysterious fetich* (sic) *– a necklace of rubies reputed to have belonged to Prester John, David penetrates a*

60

guarded stronghold, learns its secrets, falls into Laputa's hands,
escapes, settles accounts with a rascally half-caste, and at last,
after many stirring adventures, succeeds in his mission, that
brisk inclusive last sentence would surely soften the mood of
even the most jaded, flinty-hearted literary agent, scowling at
yet another synopsis amid the day's avalanche of submissions,
yes, strong, vivid characters and a racy plot – ingredients which
date back all the way from H. Rider Haggard to *Hamlet*, Homer
and Hermippus, of course what Hollis didn't see in those
childish days was that every book has an agenda, the politics of
Prester John floated past him like a wisp of cloud in a blue sky,
he never saw that the book was a celebration of empire, the
casual racism quite passed him by, take our hero's diabolical
African adversary, John Laputa, for instance, *I said he was an*
educated man, but he is also a Kaffir, He can see the first stage
of a thing, and maybe the second, but no more, That is the
native mind, that's blacks for you, they'll never be as smart as
whites, they can't help it, poor things, it's in their biology, a
message deemed suitable for young adolescent boys and girls in
Hampshire, in that era, a time when people were still being
executed by hanging in British jails, when homosexual acts
between consenting adults were a criminal offence, and when
Bobby Vee had a hit with 'Rubber Ball', a song which still echoes
in Hollis's mind, yes, if he was ever to be invited on to Desert
Island Discs – this is one of his top fantasies – rest assured that
Mr Vee would be among his amazing choices, for like Mr Vee's
synthetic orb, the old cougars in Hollis's life make him
reverberate vertically, mentally speaking, as Hollis grows older
and more decrepit and sweet memory drags him back to more
muscular days, he returns to the cougars, they are absent now –
some – most – all – are indubitably dead – but they live on, as
spectres do, enough! on Saturday afternoons Dirk pedalled
round on his bicycle and Hollis joined him on a ride to the local
public library, on the way they stopped at a sweet shop to buy

eight ounces of candy (to use the American expression), yes, these are the days when sweet shops still exist, with row upon row of mouthwatering delights stocked in big glass bottles, the old smiling grey-haired grandfatherly shopkeeper unscrews the lid and doles out the required weight of sweeties, then they pedal on to the library, return their books and borrow more, afterwards to Dirk's house to watch the wrestling on TV, large wide stocky men with stages names like Bruiser Brown and Thrasher Torrance strapped their flab into tight leotards and engaged in choreographed clashes while emitting stage-snarls and dramatically stamping their feet, a crowd with the lowest IQ in England went wild with joy or indignation, as we watched the fun we munched our sweeties (or in my case, sucked), my particular favourite was sherbet lemons, they had an edgy flavour of citrus – a sweet biting sharp sensation which spread around the palate – and then, when you had licked and sucked away the hard yellow outer shell – a sudden ecstatic flood of sensation when the little pocket of cocaine-white sherbet was finally breached, yes, in old age – my life has been a constant quest for sensation – the nearest I can get to that sharp biting ancient pleasure is tingling chemical-sodden artisan salt and cider vinegar crisps, true, and then on Sundays I'd begin reading whatever book I'd borrowed the day before, yes, I was a keen reader and in those days my tastes depended on what was available in the library, and what riches they were! sometimes there were titles which sounded very naughty indeed and which I knew I would never have the courage to take down from the shelf and lay on the counter in front of the hawk-eyed scowling librarian who staffed it, *The Naked and the Dead*, for example, that was a title which made me shiver, I did furtively glance inside the book to see if there were any pictures but disappointingly it was just a novel, page after boring page of prose, Charles Dickens had managed to write books with illustrations but this was evidently beyond the abilities of Mr

Mailer, who was (this probably explained the deficiency) an American, he gazed at me from his author's photograph on the jacket, a pugnacious-looking curly-haired young man, never in my wildest dreams did I imagine that Mr Mailer would one day fly across the Atlantic and I would meet him face to face and get him to sign a book for me, by then, alas, he was fatter than any of the wrestlers on Saturday afternoon television – but much friendlier, yes, over the decades he had acquired the reputation of a bruiser and a wife-stabber but in the flesh, strapped into a blue blazer with gold buttons like a comic pantomime character, he was conviviality itself, a real charmer, at this point it may be helpful to recapitulate, as my history teacher Mr Edge used to say, yes, in those days the teaching of history required all pupils to adopt the skills of parrots, facts were drummed into us, along with the interpretation of those facts, we learned them by heart, as the saying is, although few of our young hearts were really in it, it was more a question of a painful duty which had to be performed in order that one Pass One's Exams, passing an exam was, we were led to believe, as important as passing a bowel motion, one ingested historical facts in the same way one ate an apple, it was good for you, it led to satisfactory results, yes, parrotting facts, I eventually discovered, is a futile endeavour, but recapitulation is not to be sneezed at, in that spirit let me recapitulate and remind the class where we have reached, pay attention at the back, this is the history narrative you all need to remember: eleven, transcendence; twelve, soup; thirteen, survey woman, I remind you of this simply to make the point that some years have, so to speak, climaxes, whereas others are as dull as proverbial ditchwater, which as we nowadays know from wildlife programmes with underwater cameras is not dull at all but seething with animated life and strange exotic vegetation, so let me start again, some years nothing much happens, there are no climaxes whatever, apart of course from those brief boiling disturbances which trouble adolescents, or to put it another way there is nothing much to report about the next two years, apart from Uncle Alfred's death from lung cancer, as I've already said – pay attention at the back – I was not allowed to go to the funeral, which meant I had an entire day to myself, while my parents attended to the ritual of burial, I celebrated the ascension, there were several risings that day, I think I was in a hurry, anxious to squeeze in as much as possible, just in case the Grim Reaper should come calling for someone else in the family, of course on those rare long days alone I was always hoping that Survey Woman would return, but she never did, in fact no one doing a survey ever again rang our doorbell, so pausing respectfully a moment to remember Uncle Alfred's friendly face and his yellow fingers and that attractive smell of cigarette smoke which created a memorable aroma around his geniality, let's slip twenty-four tedious months and get on to some action in a year when I had two summer holidays, two adventures, here's my first, in the fifth form, I'd become very good friends with a boy I'll call Dennis Wilkins, he lived in Southsea, some weekends I would catch the number 33 double-decker bus to visit him at his home overlooking the Solent, we'd go swimming together from the unpleasantly shingly beach, afterwards we'd head off on a bike ride and then finally go back to his house and chew liquorice sticks and suck aniseed balls and play Monopoly, good clean innocent fun which left one with nothing but black teeth, Dennis was ginger-haired, with a very freckly face, his mother, Brenda, also had a freckly face, his father, Harold, did not have freckles, Harold's face was lobster-pink and plump, as parents they were quite friendly, if a little distant, but Brenda Wilkins was always generous with the coconut creams, what I was not expecting – Dennis hadn't warned me – was that in the morning she'd bring me a cup of tea in bed, I remember it well, their guest room was warm and summery, outside a blackbird was singing its cheery song, *cheepy-cheepy-cheep-cheep!* I was in my standard matutinal position, half-awake, pleasantly drowsy, I'd pushed down the bedspread and the sheets, I lay on my back, I was in Africa, stroking a giraffe, and then I was in the jungle, strangling a python, the risen sun had filled the green curtains with a blaze of colour, my eyes closed, into my mind floated Elsie Burton of the Lower Sixth, she descended like a hot air balloon, curvaceous, swaying, and then phantom Elsie burst like a balloon, shredded by a spatter of sound, a cough, a rasping, double-spurted cough, phlegm brought up from the depths of a throat and ejaculated, twice, cough-cough, a double cough, in quick succession, a cough that said: *there's someone else in my bedroom!* I opened my eyes, the door stood, wide open, beyond the figure standing in its frame I could see the house interior, as static, tranquil and resonant as a painting by Vermeer, a grandfather clock ticked like a bomb in a James Bond film, a tall mirror cast a hexagon of yellow sunlight on the pale rug, a luminous light made everything seem to glow: the Dresden shepherdess in a blue bonnet, the seated Cornish pisky with its bronze knees pointing upward, the transparent tube containing different coloured layers of sand from Alum Bay, in the foreground, framed by the doorway, stood a frozen figure, it was Dennis's freckled mother, Brenda, lost in my reverie I had not heard her open the door, and now she stood there, in her dressing gown, holding a cup of tea, and staring, staring, staring, Mrs Wilkins, I said, in a voice of stone, I felt a deep violent blush surge across my face with the concentrated intensity of the Severn Bore, my hand jerked as if stung by a passing wasp, Mrs Wilkins continued to stare at me, Hollis Block, she said, in a soft, silky, surprised voice, she closed the door behind her and came into the room, she put the cup of tea down on the dressing table, for some reason her hand was a little shaky that morning and the cup rattled on its saucer, she moved towards me until she loomed over me like an accusing angel, sent by a Lord who felt that in this lamentable matter enforcement was long overdue, or so I felt at that moment, Goodness, she said, she stood above me, not moving, gazing down, she put the cup of tea down, Goodness, she repeated, I made a sort of gargling, strangled sound, no words shot from between my lips, they were moist, and my tongue, another stalk of flesh which had a life of its own, seemed to be moving across them, backwards and forwards, to and fro, she leaned over me, smelling faintly of bacon, saying nothing she undid the belt of her floral dressing gown, beneath it she was naked, she let the gown swing open, she had big freckled breasts and further down there thrived a rich wild ginger like a rare bush which had been carefully nurtured under glass at Kew, she smiled, then drew the gown across that spectacle, as she did so she released a single stupendous fart, it was like a thunderclap, I half-expected my teacup to crack or for the wardrobe to shake, its pungent aroma seemed to flood the room, surely the sound of that involuntary explosion had been heard all over the house, like a bird responding to another bird's signal a voice called Brenda! Where are you?, she turned round, raised the hem of the gown and bent over, giving Hollis a quick glimpse of her bottom, a magnificent structure, plump, pale, fabulously curved, and that gingery mass bridging where her body bifurcated, Hollis could have stared at that view forever, and as the gown slid further he saw her naked back, it was coated with freckles! hundreds of them! a galaxy of freckles! but then she at once stood again, hid her treasures, she tightened the belt, at the door she stood looking back at him, Drink your tea, Hollis, she said, Hurry up, or will it get cold, and don't be late for breakfast, I won't, Mrs Wilkins, she nodded, smiled, and went out, yes, Hollis has never ceased to marvel at the wiles and deceits of Woman, not once did Mrs Wilkins ever allude to what had occurred between us, that night he half-expected the door to his bedroom to creak open, a large, curvaceous figure would tiptoe across the threadbare carpet, remove her dressing gown, and slip into bed with him, to slip him inside her, that never happened, nor, when she brought me my tea the next morning, did she do anything but put the cup and saucer down and wish Hollis good morning, he was lying under the eiderdown, engorged with expectation, the eiderdown had been pressed upward into a shape which greatly resembled the great pyramid of Giza, Hollis was stunned and deeply disappointed when she simply put the cup of tea down on his bedside table and walked out of the room, the next morning – which was his last one – he made a special point of being prepared for her entry, on this occasion she simply glanced down at him and said in a brisk, half-annoyed voice, Oh *do* cover yourself up Hollis, yes, how inconstant is Woman! his pre-breakfast surprise that first memorable morning was strictly a one-off and after it, when he entered the breakfast room Mrs Wilkins was her usual self, she displayed not the slightest sign of guilt or embarrassment or anxiety that he might advert to the recent past, to what had occurred, no, no one could ever have suspected what had happened, the only clue to what had occurred ten minutes earlier was possibly a slightly deeper shade of pink on her cheeks and a strange ambiguous sparkle in her dark green eyes, two years later the Wilkins family moved again, to Brighton, Dennis left for another school, Hollis corresponded intermittently and a year later he had a letter from Dennis to tell him that his parents were getting divorced, his mother had left them to live with a fireman, Dennis was living with his father, Hollis wrote back to say he was sorry to hear about that and to tell him the latest news about Pudney Park County High School, Dog-Ends and Welshie had been suspended! they'd had a punch-up in the staff room! the rumour was that they might both get the sack! and there was more good news, Mr Belcher had been very badly burned down one leg when a boy, Smith, a second year, had accidentally tipped a beaker of acid over him, Dennis wrote back wanting to hear more, I duly replied, but then later that year he stopped replying to my letters and finally we lost touch altogether, this is the same year that my father buys his first car, he is fifty years old and, by the standards of the times, reasonably affluent, my parents are emergent working-class and I am the first fruits of their brave emergence, I am born incipiently middle-class, I shall have what they never enjoyed – a university education, yes, out there, things are looking good for the English, the economy is booming, Empire Day has been abolished but we still have colonies, housewives are now blessed with washing-machines, it is the dawn of mass car ownership but it will take another twenty years before a car starts to seem essential for every family, at this point in the nation's history bicycle sales remain high and many middle-class people cycle to work, you see it at the end of the movie *Genevieve* when the hero and heroine reach London, they drive through streets full of cyclists, for the British working class cycling is still the only method of personal propulsion faster than walking, you can witness it at the start of the movie, *Saturday Night and Sunday Morning*, you might almost be in China! yes, Our First Car, it is strange that there are no paintings of this crucial moment in family life in the early sixties, I have never forgotten that vehicle, though it must long ago have been broken down into scrap, melted down, and ended up as something else, a washing-machine drum, perhaps, our car is a Hillman Minx, registration number URV 17, nowadays, my mind slowly collapsing like the rusted supports of a condemned pier, I struggle to remember my PIN numbers, and every supermarket check-out is an obstacle where I risk public humiliation, but that registration number, like a first love, I have never forgotten, the colour of our Minx is avocado green – a shade which will later become fashionable for bathrooms – I will not actually see or taste an actual avocado for another eleven years, when I am introduced to the pleasures of its flesh by a girl called Honey, yes, a car means freedom, with a car you can go where you want to, and in this golden era there is free parking everywhere, the streets are largely empty, there are no yellow lines or poles bearing signs with listed restrictions, there are no traffic wardens, there are no seat-belts, no head rests, no retractable wing mirrors, having acquired our freedom to go anywhere my parents had decided we should spend our summer holiday in Scotland, beep-beep! off we go! it took my father five days to drive there, in those days the Great North Road was the fastest route, we stopped off one night to stay with obscure northern relations in Yorkshire, they spoke funny, they really did say things like *ee bah gum*, if my parents had brought me up in this region I too would have ended up speaking in a peculiar dialect which immediately marked me down as from oop north, this would only have helped if I'd wanted to write realist novels telling tales of gritty working-class life, this option held no appeal, who now remembers or reads Stan Barstow? the other nights on that long slow voyage towards the barbarian tip of Great Britain we spent in bed-and-breakfast establishments, I distinctly remember the one in Perth, it had scores of midges clinging to a ceiling disfigured by overlapping brown rings, like a tablecloth covered in coffee-cup stains, but this might have been on our return south, most of that journey is a blur, I sat on the back seat reading a Sanders of the River book from the library, more gripping adventure with a large residue of racism and colonialism, not that I noticed, I was with Sanders all the way, as he brought peace to a troubled, anarchic land, Africans are hot-blooded people, they needed the cool detachment of the white man to calm them down and bring order and justice, when it rained or when I was tired I crawled under a tartan blanket, made a pillow of my cardigan, and snoozed across the back seat, there were no seat belts in those days, no, there are only two quick ways by automobile into the Highlands: via Edinburgh or via Glasgow, my father chose Glasgow, before we reached what in those days was a city every bit as dismal as Portsmouth (no, *worse*) we stopped off at a B & B in a little place called Lockerbie, I remember nothing about it, Lockerbie was the kind of place where it was obvious nothing of significance had ever happened and nothing ever would, next morning we drove on, it was grey and overcast, after passing through the complicated road network of vast slate-grey hellish Glasgow – at a later date when I worked my way through Dante's greatest hit in the Dorothy Sayers translation I suddenly realised why the terrain seemed vaguely familiar – we at last reached the Highlands, greenery was everywhere, framing vast stretches of dark gleaming water, and big bare mountainsides which soared up towards the sky, some still had scraps of snow scattered about their tops, like bits of paper dropped by a giant, but enough Style, let the camera swivel and focus on a teenage face as Hollis stares out of the side window of the Minx, entranced, they came to Loch Lomond, the sun came out, it was like that moment in *The Pilgrim's Progress* when Christian, having successfully negotiated the Slough of Despond and all the other obstacles, finally reaches the Delectable Mountains, it was nice, very nice, the weather had indubitably perked up, the sun casts its light over pine forests and purple heather, the bonnie banks glowed, it was as if Nature was harnessing every cliché of the nascent Scottish tourist industry, back then at the roadside there were even bagpipers, men in kilts with all the accessories, they loitered in lay-bys, when you stopped to visit an adjacent signposted picturesque Falls or even just for a quick trip into the trees to relieve an aching bladder – Scottish highways seemed utterly lacking in public lavatories – they would jerk into life and begin their caterwauling, yes, these scarlet-costumed musicians were soliciting tips, beep-beep! and on we went, along the winding shoreline road, I knew about this loch from the famous song, I little knew that just twelve years later I'd be travelling along this same route with black-haired merry-eyed Militká Lazarová, yes, even at my advanced age the memory of it still makes me shiver, beep-beep! And now Loch Lomond evaporates and the trees fall away, now the mountains crowd closer and there is only rock and desolation, the sun has long since been dimmed then completely obscured by a sliding belly of cloud, it gets darker and darker, we have reached Glencoe, I press my nose to the window and gaze at its stark unending beauty, it is most unlike Bungalow-Land, it is a bit like being inside that ace poem by Robert Browning, a one-time giant of Eng Lit nobody reads any more, mountains and desolation and the shadowy presence of death: *Dauntless, the slug-horn to my lips I set, / And blew 'Childe Roland to the Dark Tower came'*, one of the best endings to any English poem, ever, I wondered if Browning had been on holiday to Scotland when he wrote it, look! there is mist around the mountain-tops and mist oozing out of the side-valleys, there is another belt of mist in the distance, directly up ahead, we are moving towards it, and now rain starts to spatter on the Minx's roof and splatter the windows, soon we are driving through torrential rain at a speed of 15mph, my father struggles to see the road ahead, luckily there are no other cars on the road at all, you can drift in your lane without fear of consequences, now we are enveloped in mist and moving at barely more than a walking pace, take it from me, a lot of Scotland is like this, misty and wet, with nothing to see for miles but bare mountains and rocks and small foaming streams rushing down hillsides, the water gurgles, the sound of Scotland – if nations were defined by distinctive sounds – would be gurgling – the sound of something liquid and lumpy as grief, being forced into a place too small to contain it (no wonder the Scots invented bagpipes), an eternity later we reached civilisation of sorts, a dismal settlement named Fort William, this strange name conjures up a wooden stockade and guards with rifles eyeing the distance for Red Indians but disappointingly it reminded me of Havant in Hampshire, a row of shops, not very interesting, here we stopped for lunch, it was still raining, I ate a peculiar spicy meat pie, with baked beans and fried onion, I was permitted a bottle of Coca-Cola, with a striped paper straw, we were on holiday, living it up, beep-beep!

And now we have reached the western end of the Great Glen, a chain of lakes, they exist to catch all the rainfall, we crawl on through the cold bitter slashing sleet, it doesn't feel like August, in Hampshire in August the crowds are boarding the Puffing Billy steam train at Havant and heading off for the hot sunlit sandy beaches of Hayling Island, cheap air fares don't exist, only the rich fly, everyone else goes to the English seaside, almost nobody goes abroad, even Scotland is an exotic destination, our next stopping place is another fort, this also lacks soldiers or a fortress, Fort Augustus is built alongside the canal, we stop at a tea-shop there, it's a much smaller place than the first fort, I rub a hole in the misted-up window and watch a boat slowly being raised up in a lock, it is getting dark, the rain seems heavier now, we run for the Minx and jump in, we head for our next B & B, just off the Inverness road, it is up a hill, beep beep! this turns out to be the steepest road we have ever driven up, the Minx's engine emits a high-pitched scream, as if it is being subjected to unbearable stress, a cloud the colour of cigarette smoke starts to rise from beneath the bonnet, my father, his face a grimace which combines determination with concentration, hunches over the steering wheel, he looks like a Spitfire pilot in one of the black and white war films I am always being taken to, Wheeee-yaaaaaaah-aaaaaagh, shrieks the Minx, Aaaaaagh! Eeeeee-aaaaagh! yet more blue smoke starts to leak out of the bonnet, the wind hurls it against the windscreen, the pungent smell of something burning fills the interior of the car, I breathe it in, my throat is burning with an acrid oily sensation, my father looks more dogged and determined than ever, a man who once drove a ten-ton truck across sand dunes in Libya (The War) isn't going to be defeated by a slope in Scotland, Charles, my mother says sharply, a single word of reproach, charged with anxiety, I sense she is all for giving up, we could go back and spend the night in Fort Augustus, there's bound to be a B & B with a room, but Charles Block is not a quitter, somehow – wheeee-yaaaaaaah-aaaaaagh! – we make it to the top of that wet dark almost vertical hill, by this time the car is full of smoke, my father stops the car and he and my mother throw their doors open, a fierce Highland gust rushes in and sweeps the fumes away, outside the light has almost gone, now we are on higher ground, alone upon a vast unending rocky plain dotted by tiny lochs, we take a few turns of the road and suddenly there is a mountain looming beside us, belts of mist drift across our path like herds of spectral bison, my father switches the headlights on, they stab the mist, we move onward, we don't meet a single vehicle all the way to our B & B, which is probably a good thing as the road has suddenly narrowed to a single track framed by drainage ditches and big granite boulders which seem to have rolled down from the crumbling crags above, yes, the night seemed to get darker and darker, the mist thicker and thicker, the road narrower and narrower, but in the end we arrived at our destination: a whitewashed house on a triangle of land between a frothing river and a small loch, our hosts were Jean and John, an affable couple whose children had left home and who were now supplementing their income by renting out rooms to summer visitors, I remember little of our arrival, I was shown to my room, I unpacked, I brushed my teeth, I said goodnight to everyone and then I went upstairs, put my pyjamas on and got into bed, we were there for four nights, I said I preferred to stay and explore the surrounding countryside while my parents went out for the day, there was a remote reservoir some forty miles away that my father wished to visit, in 1958 two flying saucers had been seen hovering over it and there was always the chance that our alien visitors might choose August for a nostalgic return visit, when they returned my father reported they'd had no luck, next day I joined them for a trip to Urquhart Castle, a tedious journey, it was another dull day, the sky full of dark cloud, nowadays the castle is a coach-clogged tourist Heritage inferno, with a large modern visitor centre and car park, today even in the urinals you can't escape the tinkling Skye Boat Song and a plastic chorus crooning Will Ye Go, Lassie, Go? but back then there was no visitor centre, and no car park, just a small lay-by suitable for at most four cars, there was no one else parked there that day, a highlander dozed on a tree stump at the roadside, as my father killed the Minx's engine the tartan-skirted scarlet-jacketed freak sprang to his feet, another bloody bagpiper! his caterwauling assaulted us as we approached the little entrance gate, my father gave him sixpence, he did not seem grateful, fierce gobbets of congested and mercifully incomprehensible language (probably Gaelic, possibly Glaswegian) accompanied us for a minute or so as we descended the long line of steps that led down a steep hill towards the castle below, my father said it was like being in Tibet, my mother nodded, she usually found it best to agree with him, we both knew father had never been to Tibet but as a much younger man he had seen the movie *Lost Horizon* and he felt that made him something of an expert on the subject, my mother, however, had vetoed his suggestion that we give our bungalow a name, she felt very strongly that apart from the local murder in a subsequently burnt out and demolished property of that name, Shangri-La was not really suitable for Hampshire, we reached the foot of the slope and crossed a narrow wooden bridge over the grassy waterless moat, a sign in the moat pointed towards an ugly concrete structure which had been installed in this grassy ditch which once held water, weeds and carp: TOILETS, my father and I hurried off to relieve our aching bladders, it was a dark malodorous place, with squares of cobweb-covered frosted glass placed high above the urinal, something fluttered in the roof as we stood in silence, making the gutter fill with amber-coloured froth, we hurried back to rejoin mother, who was loitering by a garden shed, inside which a dour woman sat knitting, she sold admission tickets, a sixpenny guide to the castle and postcards, my father declined the guide, he knew about castles, there was little he didn't know, one and six for adults, ninepence for children, my father paid and we walked past a collapsed archway and entered the castle grounds, it had been blown up centuries earlier but was still satisfyingly castle-shaped, the tower still stood and so did many of the walls, it looked just like a romantic ruined castle should do, we wandered around on the neatly trimmed grass, visited the dungeon, and climbed to the top of the tower to gaze down at the loch, from up there it seemed bigger than ever, the next day we drove to the coast to gaze at distant Skye, and after that it was on to Inverness, Culloden, I duly mounted the Cumberland stone, then Edinburgh, then back south, a new school year beckoned, I barely remember it, or the one after, I was now mercifully down to three subjects, which I had to sit for my 'A Level' exams when I was eighteen, I had chosen – or my miserable exam results at 'O Level' had chosen them for me, by a process of elimination – History, Geography and English, this last subject had two components – language and literature, language bored me, literature was intermittently interesting but nowhere near as good as the fiction of Dennis Wheatley, Wordsworth was OK but his verse and his Lake District were not as good as *The Island Where Time Stands Still*, Gerard Manley Hopkins had some memorable lines but none so memorable as that sentence in one of Wheatley's thrilling works: 'He found the place and thrust', what adolescent boy could not but feel a frisson of excitement as Wheatley's lusty hero Roger Brook brought a truculent, voluptuous, exotic foreign beauty to heel, but nothing compared to a new author I'd discovered, whose fiction supplied such electrifying chapter titles as 'Dynamite from Nightmare-Land', 'Then I Began to Scream' and 'The Crash of Guns', yes, Ian Fleming was a tip-top writer, even though *The Spy Who Loved Me* wasn't like any of the others in the 007 series, being narrated by a girl called Viv, but it had an unforgettable moment of interrupted intercourse in a cinema, I've never forgotten that scene, whereas I've read *War and*

Peace and, frankly, nothing lingers in the mind, as for History: boring, but Geography... the Geography teacher was an enthusiastic young Scotsman, whom the class promptly nick-named Jock (Jock the pupil had long since departed with his parents, back across the border, England didn't suit them), we liked Jock, who, compared with the rest of the teaching staff, seemed human, he must have been about thirty, he didn't shout, he didn't lose his temper, he seemed quite affable, his Scottish accent was so weak he could be understood at all times, plus he took us on trips out of school, at a time when the only sanctioned release from an eight-year stretch in Pudney Prison was to study Geography for 'A Level', the syllabus included a large component of geomorphology, that craggy topic required field trips, we had days out, by coach, taking a packed lunch and a notebook, to understand how water could shape chalk we visited the site of Corfe Castle, to see how wave action could affect limestone we took a trip to Durdle Door, to learn the effects of groundwater on sandstone and limestone we visited Wookey Hole, best of all, to understand glaciation we had a week in the Lake District, staying at the Youth Hostel in Keswick, I remember best the ascent of Red Pike, high above Buttermere, I returned south with a much better understanding of what a tarn was and terminal moraine and how to recognise drumlins, drumlins were my favourite landscape form, Freudists can guess why, luckily the Lake District trip involved lots of walking, leaving me exhausted, I had to share a room with a boy called David, he was deaf in one ear, we got along alright but we were never really friends, the years pass, as a child I had wept while reading *Black Beauty* and now I was reading *Horse Under Water*, this book was not about a quadruped, it was the latest paperback spy thriller by a current favourite author of mine, 'Horse' was slang for heroin, some sort of drug, I had heard of drugs and knew they were Very Bad but my knowledge of intoxicants at this moment in my life was restricted to a small weekly glass of cider with mother's Sunday chicken, I still remember, I still remember that paperback, yes, in old age I am a lost soul with rotting teeth and tumbling grey hair who still haunts second-hand bookshops, there are fewer and fewer of these establishments left nowadays, visiting them I feel like Winston Smith exploring a forbidden zone for mementoes of the past, anything to trigger a memory, Ah, Winston Smith! another protagonist in a condition of advanced physical decay, Winston is younger than I am now, too, but I don't have varicose veins, and Winston proves to be irresistibly (inexplicably!) attractive to raunchy Julia, yes, *Nineteen Eighty-Four* is a novel to give hope to all repellent, decaying old men, yes, second-hand bookshops are strange, dark places, cramped as the womb but full of silence, a silence in which all you can hear is your own thumping blood, so many of the old familiar paperbacks of yesteryear are there in these dusty temples to the abandoned ones, they line up, with twisted spines, like pensioners queuing for their free winter 'flu injection, take one down off the shelf and see how it is as wrinkled and blotchy as anyone older than sixty, an old paperback doesn't lie or deceive or conceal, an old paperback can't wear a scarf to hide a scraggy neck, or a pair of gloves to conceal that loathsome assemblage of liver spots, an old paperback doesn't apply vampire-scarlet to cracked, ancient lips or coat its decay in powder as white as snow, *The Constant Nymph* originally priced at three shillings and sixpence, *Horse Under Water* for five shillings, on the back we learn that young Londoner Len Deighton has rocketed into the ranks of international best-selling authors *but not without a storm of controversy*, Len Deighton, according to *Newsweek,* makes *Brave New World* and *1984* look like 'the good old days', *LIFE* magazine offers up: *Next, big soft girls will read Len Deighton aloud in jazz workshops*, you wouldn't dare to say that nowadays, would you? a million tweets would denounce this as sexist, and it would definitely make Pseuds Corner in *Private*

Eye, yes, those were the days my friend, also for five bob: *Across the River and Into the Trees*, what a marvellous cover this last title has, a white bust of Hemingway, with a mandolin resting against his skull and in the foreground a silver wine bucket containing a bottle of Deutz champagne, propped between the bottle and the rim of the bucket is a postcard of a Canaletto painting of the Piazza San Marco and the Campanile, in the foreground is a champagne glass of the period (shallow and bowl-shaped, made of cut glass), before modernity arrived in the form of the flute, wedged between this glass and the silver flank of the bucket is a one-hundred Lira banknote, propped against Hemingway's chest is the framed portrait of a girl, over which is draped a turquoise pendant, the left corner of the picture frame is pressed against the neck of a dead mallard, this deceased duck rests on a monochrome photograph of a young man in uniform – perhaps Hemingway himself – upon which lie three medals, between the star-shaped medal on the right lies a small glass bottle, the stopper has been removed and some of its contents spill out – turquoise-coloured amphetamines in capsule form, you don't get covers like that on modern paperbacks, next *A Sea of Troubles* (OPEC has put up the price of oil and inflation has kicked in – a Penguin now costs six shillings), by Marguerite Duras, author of *Hiroshima Mon Amour*, no reviews are cited on the jacket, just a publisher's blurb, holding out the delights *of the vivid authenticity and superb economy of style of her later and very distinguished novels* **Moderato Cantabile** *and* **The Square**, yes, how now forgotten is the ancient stimulation embedded in that era of paperback book covers, yes, it was a golden age for female nudity – a last summer before a bleak, puritan feminism swept like winter across the publishing houses of this ancient isle, snuffing out the sales potential of voyeurism, a time when for five shillings you could snap up Nelson Algren's new paperback *Notes From a Sea Diary: Hemingway All The Way*, a heartfelt tribute to the recently self-extinguished writer, it takes the form of an autobiographical account of a voyage on a freighter to Pusan, Kowloon, Bombay and Calcutta, spliced with tales of Algren's descent into an underworld of bars, thieves, prostitution and men 'gone bamboo' (marvellous expression!) are reflections on Hemingway as man and writer, it bears – bares! – one of the most erotic book covers a teen could hope to come across (a phrase which within hours of purchase will in some hands take on a quite literal meaning, smiley-face), yes, it's a photograph, we see a naked black woman's back and a white man who is holding her against him, the image has been cropped, we do not see their heads, we see the white man's forearms and the backs of his partly outspread hands, we can see that the white man is wearing trousers because there's the silhouette of one of his belt loops, the black woman is obviously hugging the white man in the same way that he is hugging her, close, we can imagine her breasts pressed against his chest, this couple are seen from a position which allows the exposure of the black woman's naked bottom, it swells up and out, beautifully curved, utterly voluptuous, yes, the erotic epicentre of this cover, surely, is the line separating that pair of ivory cheeks, the photographer having cunningly angled a light in his studio so that it illumines the base of her spine and the crests of those swelling curves, the black curving slit between them arcs downward and melts into darkness, where imprecision lurks, the imagination thrives, who cannot conceive of that chasm opening up to provide access to a pit of shuddering wonders, even better it's just a book, one can cunningly sandwich it between a volume of poems and a history of Tudor England, a fellow's mother will never realise it's dual purpose, yes, what a gorgeous era this was for paperbacks, *The Function of the Orgasm* comes out (again, no pun) in paperback! only nine shillings and sixpence for a scientific analysis of life's most important gift! I read the blurb: *There is a growing impression (shared, for instance, by such writers as Norman Mailer,*

William Burroughs, and Clellon Holmes), that, poetically,
Reich has something very important to tell us, you bet, Reich's
basic message was that orgasms are very good for you, you
should try to have as many as possible (although a pitch should
surely be made for the added benefits of a daily teaspoon of cod
liver oil with one's breakfast tea, lots of fibre in your breakfast
cereal and an apple every lunchtime), all of this, over a forty-
year stretch, can virtually guarantee a record of achievement
which stands at 19,638 orgasms (adding nocturnal emissions
makes 19,969), yes, *Clellon Holmes*, a puzzle, Hollis had never
encountered or read anything by Clellon Holmes, in fact he had
never heard of her, it turned out that Clellon was a man, which
surprised him, as Clellon seemed a female sort of name, or
possibly that of a space-monster, but he was an American, which
explained it, many Americans have the most peculiar names,
what sort of a name is 'Chip', yes, Clellon Holmes was a close
friend of Jack Kerouac but nowhere near as famous, he wrote a
novel about jazz, which was greatly admired by people who –
toot-toot wah-wah be-doopy-doo-wah-zzzeeeby bo-wah-wah-
zatoot-toooooot – like novels about jazz, John Clellon Holmes
also wrote a New York novel, *Go*, which is a thinly disguised
account of the life of the beat heroes including Jack Kerouac and
Neal Cassady and Allen Ginsberg before they became famous, it
is about drugs, wild parties and what used to be called *free love*,
Hollis wished he had heard about this book earlier in his life,
when it might have excited him, but by now it was too late, yes,
that phrase *free love* always reminded him of the scene in *The*
Spy Who Came in from The Cold – the movie, not the book –
when Richard Burton describes his relationship with Claire
Bloom, She offered me free love, he says, adding dryly: at the
time it was all I could afford, very droll, as for William
Burroughs, Hollis had once seen him, he came to a literature
event in Cheltenham, nowadays, of course, even the most
miserable town in this rainswept land can conjure up an arts

week, featuring a BBC celebrity plugging their book, a septuagenarian band which once had a hit around 1963, a minor crime novelist promoting their fifth book about the adventures of Chief Inspector Lucy Crisp, and Jo Gasp, a gibbering, hair-jerking, verbally incontinent performance poet, if you are really lucky the septuagenarian band will cancel at the last moment owing to the singer suffering a stroke and the drummer requiring an urgent knee replacement, making way for a last minute Roy Orbison impersonator – fat, balding but with some really cool shades and not such a a bad voice after all, *Priddy woomannnn... It's ohhhhhh-vurrrrr...* but I digress, at a time when literary fairs and arts weeks and the Hay Festival did not yet exist some bright spark in Cheltenham had organised a meeting of minds, three then marginal novelists were brought together to discuss the modern novel, one of them was William Burroughs, I had read *Naked Lunch*, which I found rather heavy going but not without excitements, thumbs-up for Mr Burroughs, was he related to Edgar Rice I wondered, by another astonishing coincidence William Burroughs is also a character in *Go*, where he is named Will Dennison! the other two writers were Brian Aldiss and B. S. Johnson, Brian Aldiss wrote science fiction, I was never awfully keen on sci-fi, although I read a bit, at the age of ten I had been entranced by *Mariners of Space*, about a top space ranger named Colin who operates out of the vast Space Port of Croydon, all aboard for the Stratosphere, the fields of Croydon dropped away as the space liner *Theian* belched white jet propulsion gases from her flange exhausts, *By twirling a tiny knob beneath his velocity indicator, Colin could tune in to any tiny vibration, eerie cracklings and rustlings came over his televiser, Colin twisted his Accelerator Knob to 1,000mph,* wheeeee! yes, Colin has to go to Mars, having discovered that Martians are behind all the problems in the world – strikes, wars, and so on, Colin saves the world, assisted by Jimmy Smith, an Ealing Studios cockney, Colin disables the Robot Army of

Mars with his ray-gun, Smith ejaculates as he bumps his head, thanks to his training Colin manages to keep a firm grip on himself, but a powerful vibration whirrs through his body, has there been some convulsion among the nebulae? *one day our Earth historians will tell the full story of the Battle of the Firmament – that grim and decisive conflict of the Interplanetary War, they will tell how the Earth Space Fleet sailed secretly from Croydon and the met the formidable strength of the Martian and Venusian fleets combined,* for saving humanity Colin and Jimmy are rewarded with the Order of the Golden Comet and the Grand Order of the Galaxy, I was also enthralled by Dennis Wheatley's *Star of Ill-Omen*, it began as all novels should begin, it hit the ground running: *Kem Lincoln slid back the chamber of his automatic to make certain that it was working freely, snapped home a clip of bullets and repouched the weapon in his shoulder holster, he hoped that he would not have to use it,* Kem, who is an ex-Commando and a top British secret agent, also goes to Mars, he has better luck than Colin, however, as he is accompanied by the beautiful Carmen Escobar, whom he manages to spend four nights with, between the sheets – detail is sadly lacking – 'they revelled in the highest delights that youth can give' – Kem and Carmen discover that Mars is run by highly intelligent flying bee-beetles, who control an indigenous population of giants who harvest beans (yes, really), the bee-beetles are worried because the Martian reserves of water are slowly diminishing, they need to emigrate to another planet, the bee-beetles are determined to obtain the secrets of the earthling's Atom bomb, they wish to bombard Earth with Atom bombs and crush all resistance, those were the glorious days when novels represented real value for money, on top of chapters you got chapter titles, and what crackers they were! 'The Explosive Pill', 'Chamber of Horrors', 'The Last Bean', Brian Aldiss didn't enthrall me the same way, not until – lawks a mercy! – *The Hand-Reared Boy*, I'd read some of his skiffy stuff, *The Primal Urge*, for example, and *Report on Probability A*, both consumed and quickly forgotten, some books stay with you forever, most don't, and those two didn't, but then science fiction was never really my cup of tea, the genre was for twelve-year-old boys who needed something to take their minds off their acne, the genre was for boys who needed something to fill up their heads with when they had tired of playing with their Meccano set, *moi*, I had discovered far more interesting machinery to handle, and if Brian Aldiss didn't enthrall, ditto B. S. Johnson, my gateways to literature in those days were Panther paperbacks and Pans and Penguins, and Panther had put out a couple of Johnsons, he was the British Beckett, supposedly, I read *Travelling People* and *Albert Angelo*, yeah, okay I suppose, the experimentalism seemed a bit forced, *Travelling People* had three pages which were filled in with little wavy lines and what looked like a blizzard of black dust particles, these were supposed to represent loss of consciousness in a drowning man, and there were two and a half pages which were entirely black, supposed to represent... I forget, death probably, but these tricks seemed stale and shallow, Laurence Sterne got there first, and his experimentalism was epic, he laid charges along the entire length of the realist novel's narrative and then ran along it, bit by bit, gleefully blowing the whole track up, he had Irish blood, obvs, a bit demented, nothing wrong with that, mind, no, yes, Sterne's spectacular wackiness made Johnson seem a bit... timid, *I doubt if there are more than six other English novelists writing today who can match his prose*, gushed the *Western Daily Press* on the cover of *Travelling People*, an odd scrap of praise, it made you wonder who those other six were, this gush was 1963 vintage so who were the six? Graham Greene? John Braine? Kingsley Amis? Iris Murdoch? John Fowles? Muriel Spark? Lawrence Durrell? David Storey? Anthony Burgess? John le Carré? Margaret Drabble? J. G. Ballard? Doris Lessing? Richard Hughes? Evelyn Waugh? that makes fifteen, not six, and B. S. Johnson was (yah! boo! tweet-tweet!) arguably a lesser writer than any of them, as for *Albert Angelo*, the tedious trick in this book is to have a slender rectangle sliced out of pages 147 and 148 and 149 and 150, so that the reader, looking back, sees only whiteness but, looking forward, sees the thrilling words *struggled to take back his knife, and inflicted on him a mortal wound above his right eye (the blade penetrating to a depth of two inches) from which he died instantly*, on page 147 this partial sentence is preceded by Albert Angelo, the novel's main character, who is a schoolteacher, saying that he is going to invite his pupils to write an essay expressing truthfully exactly what they feel about him *with a guarantee that there will be no complaints or recriminations from me, whatever they say, with the hope that they will thereby work out their hatred of me without it actually needing to come to violence, how about that for an idea then question mark*, the ensuing white space leading the reader on towards that rectangular window, with its clear indication of imminent violence, and then, turning the page, the reader finds herself in Cablestrasse, where a punch-up breaks out and on the next page, page 149, the sentence visible through the rectangular window is preceded by the name of Johnson's character Terry, who is involved in a fight, thus: *Terry struggled to take back his knife, and inflicted on him a mortal wound above his right eye (the blade penetrating to a depth of two inches) from which he died instantly*, but then you turn the page and discover that didn't happen, it's all an authorial trick, and the words about the lethal stabbing refer to the death in Deptford of Christopher Marlowe, dramatist, cute, clever, tricksy, yawn, don't you just hate novels which are written without the letter 'e' and other dreary conjuror's tricks, I need to get back to sleep, but the cover, the cover was something else, as so often with fiction the cover was better than the matter it sandwiched, this cover was designed by the immortal Abis Sida Stribley and isn't bad, it isn't bad at all, it shows an old-fashioned school desk (exactly the sort that Hollis had at Pudney Park County High School), the drawer is pulled open, displaying a red school notebook, a comic, and a knife used for pottery and coated with flakes of dried clay, plus, much more interestingly, three black-and-white photographs of attractive young women in states of undress, in one the woman stares straight at the viewer, her skirt is pulled up and she displays a portion of the right leg's suspender, which is holding her black stocking to her knickers, if you use your imagination you might, just, be able to think you are seeing her crotch, but you aren't really, at this moment in English cultural history the photographic reproduction of pubic hair is not yet publicly available outside Soho, the photograph on the left shows a woman – perhaps the same woman – turned round, exposing her white knickers, which cling to her ample rear, there is another glimpse of a suspender belt, this image is more erotic than the first one, black stockings, bare thigh, white cotton over the contours of a curved bottom, *frabjous*, but best of all is the photograph on the right, strewth, totally topless, flaunting a perfect pair, a voluptuous fruit the juiciness of which is only accentuated by the elbow-length black gloves of the nude model, which matched her black stockings, alas! her bent fleshy left leg, cunningly positioned, obscured the dark and hairy portal to the palace of delight, yes, nothing but black ink filling a page, B. S. Johnson's characters and plots didn't really grab me, so why (you ask yourself), why did Hollis buy a ticket for three novelists he wasn't especially keen on? simply because they were novelists, who would be visible in the flesh, yes, Hollis was very keen to see an actual living novelist, because, remember, in those days a live and visible novelist was rarer than a Coelacanth, a novelist was a member of an exclusive species – a magician of the printed word, a conjuror of plots and characters – a living marvel, a recluse who at best might emerge and give an interview – but only at intervals of several years, and at this public event this trio would talk – oh glory, glory! – about novels, Hollis bought a ticket, quite what he was doing in Cheltenham he's forgotten, yes, since that magical era novelists have become as common as muck, every dreary town in Britain seems to host an arts festival, where familiar names rotate like asteroids, most writers are self-obsessed narcissists, oozing insincere charm, one or two are The Real Thing, Louis de Bernières seems like a genuinely nice fellow, Val MacDermid is a fine comic entertainer, neither (quite rightly) has any time for diet books, the late Norman Mailer our hero Hollis also saw live, but not until the adventures of this sleepless half-dreamed tale were long over, I suppose Mailer's career was also pretty much over by that time, he was in Britain promoting what is probably his worst and least-read novel, *Ancient Evenings*, a vast, sprawling brick of a book set in – of all places! – ancient Egypt, who wants to read over 800 pages of a story set long ago, when people had names like Menenhetet One? the year was 1983, Mailer was in London, doing publicity for his new book, he appeared at the I.C.A., on The Mall, in an interview session with the genial Melvyn Bragg, all I remember is that a posh woman in the audience asked Mailer why he had used 'ass' instead of 'arse' in the novel, Mailer replied that his American readership would have laughed from coast to coast, a dry genial fellow, Norm, plus it is always a smart move to put the word 'naked' in the title of a novel, it more or less guarantees attention and bestseller status, for example: *The Naked and the Dead*, still in print today, also: *Naked Lunch*, also still in print today, and let us also not forget *Naked Came The Stranger*, a Sphere paperback, the cover described it as involving *bizarre sex* and being about a woman *whose sexual appetite was insatiable*, to add to these advertised delights the blurb helpfully identified it as *one of the dirtiest books of all time*, retail price: five shillings, as for the cover... it was the kind of cover no publisher would dare to use nowadays, a naked woman with her back to the camera kneels on a fur rug, jet black hair cascades down her back, almost to the base of her spine, her right arm is stretched vertically, her hand grips a stick of lipstick, she is crossing out four vertical marks drawn on a circular gold-framed mirror, she has just added a fifth one, these marks plainly signify lovers, this is a woman on a mission, and there is space on the mirror for more men to play their allotted roles, the wall of this room is blood red, there is a hint of Francis Bacon in the composition – the expanses of plain colour, the balanced shapes of the mirror, the surge of hair, the soles of the folded feet, the contrasting horizontal strip of white fur, she might almost be kneeling on the back of a large polar bear, yes, a visually arresting display in which voluptuous curves are the central focus, hanging in space like large generous breasts, and where the curves separate, where, with better lighting, one might expect to see a dense mass of hair framing a ploughman's furrow, there is only a void of shadow, a space in which the imagination can sport like a frisky dolphin, supplying that which even this brazen publisher dared not include, yielding moments which among better-read readers might aptly be described as Borgesian, yes, so let us now emerge from a second-hand bookshop, sneezing from a recent encounter with dust, let us stumble blinking through the harsh sunlight of the north Norfolk coast and report that first editions of *Ancient Evenings*, with dustjackets in immaculate condition, are now cheaper to buy than when they first appeared in bookshops in 1984, yes, Norman Mailer's reputation has collapsed like a derelict tower-block detonated by a demolition firm, at his death there was a great puff of smoke and when it cleared his reputation was in shreds, he was a dinosaur, a chauvinist, a mediocre writer, a populist who had touched the transient temper of his times but who now seemed as irrelevant to the modern age as a penny farthing or a hula hoop, yes, yet through bruised by this assault I nevertheless bought his remaindered last novel, *The Castle in the Forest*, a fictional biography of the young Adolf Hitler, alas it was terrible, Hitler, in this version, shared many of the weirder preoccupations of our Norman's wisdom, to wit the Devil as a force in human history, satanic forces straight of out Dennis Wheatley, and psychic battlegrounds that brought back the scene in *An American Dream* in which the hero eyeballs a bad man, and they fight it out by staring at each other, when the other man finally looks away our hero has won! pitifully macho, and as I stared glumly at my long row of Norman Mailer paperbacks I felt like someone who has invested heavily in shares for a company which is now worthless, a few years later I gave them away to the local Oxfam charity shop where they remained, week after week, attracting no buyers, then, one day, they had vanished, either they'd been snapped up by a rare Mailer fan or they'd gone off to be pulped, yet there was one title I couldn't bring myself to dispose of, to this day I still have my signed first edition, *To Hollis Block from Norman Mailer*, and now the weather of my dreams changes, I am not sure where I am but I'm not hungry – it was only just gone dream-eleven – but I needed dream-coffee, I sat by a dream-window and stared out at the rainswept street, then I took out my paperback of the week, a three-and-sixpenny Panther by Elizabeth Smart: *By Grand Central Station I Sat Down and Wept*, and I am dazzled, astonished, swept away, this is how novels should be written! a torrent of poetry! the sexy young female narrator is crazily in love with a married man, who is a writer, she has offered to help him type his work, the typewriter – now an ancient item of technology as quaint and defunct as a quill pen – becomes an object of adoration, it is *his* typewriter, this is a report from the front line of female desire, in all its intensity, marvellous stuff! I sip my coffee and absorb this wondrous prose, *He has a book to be typed, but the words I try to force out die on the air and dissolve into kisses whose chemicals are even more deadly if undelivered, my fingers cannot be martial at the touch of an instrument so much connected to him, the machine sits like a*

temple of love among the papers we never finish, and if I
awake at night and see it outlined in the dark, I am electrified
with memories of dangerous propinquity, electrified, yes, I am,
I am, for who could ever have thought that a cold metal
typewriter could be so charged with so much sexual longing? I
have never read literary fiction quite as stunning as this, I
plunge deeper into this sultry, sex-saturated saga of a young
woman hungering for another woman's husband, I go on –
another scalding sip of Wimpy coffee – I must be in Inverness –
and on, and – I am skipping some years, in later adolescence I
moved out of the bungalow into a room in the garden, my father
has had builders round to construct an extension to the garage,
my new home is simply a bare brick room with a single electrical
socket, the ceiling was made of wood and the roof was flat and
covered with charcoal-coloured roofing felt, in the summer it
was a snug, warm room and in the winter it was bitterly cold
with ice forming on the windows, the floor consisted of stone
flagstones, hidden under strips of carpet and a rug, my father
grandly gave permission to paint the bare walls, he would have
done it himself but he was too busy researching The Dreamers,
The Locked-Ins and The Wild Ones, these (he explained to me,
whenever he could trap me into conversation) were the souls of
the dead, they inhabit the lowest astral plane, which is the first
of various rings or planes around the Earth, Dreamers are
unaware that they are dead and have quit their physical bodies,
they attempt to continue physical life activities during waking
hours, they imagine they are eating, drinking and going to work,
but in the middle of an action they suddenly 'wink out' and
vanish back into their soul-sleep, only to awaken later and
continue their dream existence, many years later I read
Austerlitz by W. G. Sebald and I was instantly reminded of my
father's theories of the after-life, for what else is Austerlitz but a
dead person, revisiting a sequence of strangely empty buildings,
a man inhabiting a grey mist, constantly trying to make sense of

his memories? the Locked-Ins are very similar to The Dreamers except that they take matters a stage further by attempting to re-enter their corpses, this explains the strange radiation effects sometimes seen in cemeteries as well as the Electronic Voice Phenomena recorded by paranormal investigators, in a cemetery one group of investigators recorded a voice saying: where's my stone? where's my stone? it was a youth, searching for his own grave, as for The Wild Ones, they are nothing at all to do with Marlon Brando or Lou Reed, they are far fewer in number than The Dreamers or The Locked-Ins, like them they do not know they have left the physical world but they know that something is not quite right and that they are somehow different, they realise that this frees them from restraints, obligations and commitments and express themselves in replicas of physical activity, they indulge in what my father would only describe as *bizarre and repulsive practices*, I would have liked to know more about these but my father simply flushed and looked both irritated and embarrassed when I asked him to say a little more about these activities, the point about The Wild Ones is that they are predators, they roam the planet searching for people whose character is weak, if someone has a loose or shaky personality there is a grave risk that a Wild One may 'piggyback' on that person, you are the rock and they are the clam, you are the rotting apple and they are the greedy wasp, I went back into the garden to my room beside the garage feeling a little shaky and unnerved, my father was unquestionably deranged but sometimes his madness seemed to contain sharp, tiny, penetrating shards of possibility, an astral plane full of dead people was a bonkers idea but the idea that a malignant psychic entity might use you for a piggyback ride was altogether more troubling, I could half-believe it was true, I had read with zest that ace thriller *The Ka of Gifford Hillary* – about a man who is murdered and who survives on the astral plane – anyone who has ever read Dennis Wheatley knows that there are invisible forces out there, waiting to pounce, no one who has read Wheatley will ever again casually dispose of their toenail cuttings, yes, The Wild Ones were troubling, perhaps a chronic addiction to pleasure wasn't a young man's fault, perhaps this young man had been piggybacked, someone from another world was at work on Hollis, yes, in the end I painted three of the walls of my garden room sky blue, on the fourth wall I paid my tribute to the current fashion for psychedelia, a fashion which extended to book covers, at a time when anthologies of beat poetry displayed bright coloured bands of dazzling abstraction which, if stared at intently, with a concentrated and enduring focus, soon began to shimmer and become three dimensional, it may have been the fumes from the mixture of old tins of house paint and bicycle paint I was using, I got to work on my walls (as Kafka might have said), swirling orange and scarlet shapes – half leaves, half tongues of fire – rose up from the floor to the ceiling, they flanked my dream woman, whom I painted as possessing a slim face buried in a mass of long golden hair, her eyes were as big as oranges, she gazed at me inscrutably when I went to bed and when I woke up in the mornings, I felt I was living inside the Donovan song 'Colours', a glorious time, I came across for the first time 'somewhere I have never travelled' by e. e. cummings – for my money the best love poem ever written – and it was the era of Faber paperbacks, with glued spines that eventually dried-up and cracked and no longer held the pages together, making every book seem like an experimental product by B. S. Johnson, so that *The Waste Land* could be read in a variety of sequences, some seeming superior to the original, T. S. Eliot, a rum cove, the poet went out early in the morning of 10 January 1957 and never came back, concealing from his flatmate John Davy Hayward with whom he had lived for eleven years that he'd slipped off to marry his secretary, Valerie, who was 38 years younger than him, FABER AND FABER of 24 Russell Square, London, I knew that address, I had tracked it down, to see the exact spot where T. S. Eliot had stood by the front door in a famous photograph, the poet has a jaunty swagger, his body slightly tilted as he leans back against a walking stick (or is it a very tightly rolled brolly?), he's wearing a double-breasted suit, tightly buttoned, gleaming spats, his left hand clutches a book (*The Waste Land and Other Poems*?) (or perhaps merely a packet of correspondence), he looks happy, and now there's a plaque at this very spot, T. S. ELIOT POET AND PUBLISHER WORKED HERE FOR FABER & FABER 1925-1965 and now I was being taught by Edgar Dunlop, a D. H. Lawrence fan, he'd even grown a beard to mimic his hero, it suited him, he was skinny and he did strangely resemble Lawrence, the downside was that our class had to wade through *The Rainbow* and *Women in Love*, this was a time when English studies were still shadowed by a towering figure called F. R. Leavis, who today is largely forgotten, his predictions of future greatness for certain contemporary writers having not entirely worked out, no, Ronald Bottrall is not now regarded as one of the greatest poets of the twentieth century, but for many years F. R. Leavis was The Man, he inspired generations of academics and English teachers, and Leavis was a Lawrence fan, oddly, he regarded literature as necessary for good moral and intellectual health and Lawrence as particularly nutritious, if you dined on *The Rainbow* you'd become A Better Person, most peculiar, when you dug deeper, the first shock was to discover that Lawrence deplored masturbation, he compared it to going to the cinema, both activities involved a foul and repellent abuse of body and intellect abasing themselves in fantasy, the second discovery was that it was screamingly obvious that Lawrence was bisexual and deeply in denial about his gay self, nude male wrestling between friends – I mean, *please* – not to mention his fascination with the anus (let's not go there), thirdly, it is surely plain that all that tosh about blood knowledge and the need for a strong leader would have led Lawrence ineluctably towards fanboy enthusiasm for the new German Chancellor and his Italian chum, but luckily for Dave he snuffed it before those loud, sexy swaggering gangsters of ambition rocked up in their sexy leather gear, he was fortunate enough to check out before he fell into the Ezra Pound category, yes, I felt that neither *Women in Love* nor *The Rainbow* were as good as the Ken Russell film adaptations, I moved on, my tastes were changing, I stumbled upon a Penguin paperback, it had a weird cover, Mexican art, the novel was called *Under the Volcano*, I wondered if the title was some sort of retort to Thomas Hardy's cosy rural idyll *Under the Greenwood Tree*, I still wonder that, but since Lowry is sixty-five-years dead it's too late to ask him, reading *Under the Volcano* for the first time is an overwhelming experience, I was bludgeoned by the prose – it was a huge coloured cloud, full of flashing lights and strange conversation and music, yes, a story set in Mexico on a single day in 1938, the last day in the life of an alcoholic minor diplomat, a British Consul named Geoffrey Firmin, a hero reviewing his life when his adulterous wife returns to him unexpectedly, it's basically *Ulysses* recycled by a romantic, a life in the day of a cuckold, but whereas Joyce was coolly detached from his creation, trying out prose style after prose style with methodical calm, Lowry was full-blooded, engaged, intoxicated and intoxicating, I am rushing on through its pages, through my back pages, I'm missing out the American girl, the girl with short hair in the office where I worked, the French girl, the librarian, I want to get on to Cleo, it was a new university, it was chic, it had halls of residence shaped like ziggurats, which won architectural awards, Sir Kenneth Clark included the university in his television series 'Civilisation', I felt like Charles Ryder being invited to Brideshead, I came from Bungalow-Land and now I was mixing with the aristocracy, I acquired a girlfriend (or did she acquire me?), a beauty with jet-black hair that came down to her waist, she was both voluptuous and posh, she had witchy, wonderful eyes, Cleo Russell was her name, *Cleo* – a name that has never quite lost its magic for me, she was remotely related to the philosopher Bertrand Russell, her mother was Lady Mary Lavinia Rose Russell, there may have been hyphens I've forgotten, her father, Lord Henry Russell, had died a decade earlier, he was a Liberal, Lady Mary was a devout Catholic, the family home was in a charming village in the Cotswolds, Cleo had a brother, Jesse, who was away at Cambridge and a sister, Eleanor, who was married to a famous journalist on the *Daily Telegraph*, the journalist – let's call him Ambrose Roar – was a household name, he was balding, with provocative right-wing opinions, he deplored coloured immigration and was keen to bring back the noose, *Daily Telegraph* readers loved him, my father considered him an exceptionally intelligent man, with a firm understanding of everything that had gone wrong in Britain, he wrote Ambrose several letters but the journalist must have been a very busy man for he never replied, Ambrose Roar died quite suddenly and unexpectedly five years after my first trip to the Russell family home, it then emerged – the story was broken by *The News of the World* – that he had been a regular client at child brothels in Thailand, upon learning the news his stricken widow became a nun at an enclosed Benedictine order in remotest Norfolk, but all this occurred long after my relationship with Cleo had ended, and besides, I never met the man, Lady Mary was tall and slender and elegant and devout, years later when I saw Claire Bloom on TV in *Brideshead Revisited* I was instantly reminded of her, I saw now where Cleo's high cheekbones came from, Lady Mary dressed in grey and black, with a jet necklace which supported a silver crucifix, the crucifix seemed to embody some kind of Celtic influence, with a pattern of twists and curls like ivy, Lady Mary, although incredibly old (she was somewhere in that grey dead zone beyond the fiftieth year), was a beautiful woman, though there was something both self-absorbed and pained about her, a grief seemed to pin back her feelings, she still missed her dead husband, Lord Henry, Cleo had a black Volkswagen car and a white horse which she stabled at Stiffkey, she was the only girl at the University who had brought her horse with her, soon after we became an item she drove me out there to meet her beloved Crunchy, she took it for a canter along the salt marshes, then returned to where I stood, cold and a little bored, now it was my turn, I had never met a horse before, Crunchy was startlingly big when you got close to him, I was duly helped to board this monster, and off Crunchy and I went, I was terrified, I was now slumped over a massive beast over which I plainly had no control whatever, luckily Crunchy was in a good mood, he galloped a hundred yards along the gritty shore of the lumpy marshland, then stopped when Cleo shouted his name, then he turned and went slowly back to his mistress, I got off the horse, trembling, aware that I had had a narrow escape from serious injury or perhaps even early extinction, since that terrible day I have kept well away from large quadrupeds, you may keep your exotic holidays, you will never tempt me up on to a camel or aboard an elephant, after that day I was always happy to let Cleo drive up to Stiffkey on her own, while I remained behind reading a book, having met her horse it was now time to meet her mother, the family home was in a little Cotswold village, above it loomed Bredon Hill, a name which I knew from a melancholy poem by A. E. Houseman, although Cleo had always referred to Barley House as 'a cottage', it turned out to be a substantial Georgian property, with five bedrooms, standing in two acres of land near the village church, it had a drive, a lawn dotted with willows, and various outbuildings at the rear, beyond the apple orchard, its proximity to an Anglican church was not an advantage to a Catholic family, there was also the matter of the church bells, they were automated and rang every fucking hour, Cleo had explained beforehand that there could be no possibility of me sleeping in her bedroom at Barley House, her mother, although of liberal tendencies, could not tolerate flagrant immorality under her own roof, the Pope would not have liked it, I had to sleep in Cleo's absent brother Jesse's bedroom, on the ground floor, its window looked out on to a wall of rhododendrons, it was a warm, cosy room with a fireplace, floral wallpaper, a single bed with crisp cotton sheets and a creamy eiderdown, there was a bedside lamp, a small bookcase crammed with paperbacks, my eyes roamed greedily over rows of Jesse's bright-spined paperback treasures: Laurie Lee's *Cider With Rosie*; Peter De Vries, *Tunnel of Love*; Erle Stanley Gardner, *The Case of the Howling Dog*; Helen Eustis, *The Horizontal Man*; *The Buildings of England: Middlesex*; Raymond Chandler, *The Big Sleep*; Norman Douglas, *Siren Land*; Ludwig Bemelmans, *Hotel Splendide*; *The Pelican Book of British Herbs*; Ernest Hemingway, *Men Without Women*; Mary Macaulay, *The Art of Marriage*; Evelyn Waugh, *Vile Bodies*, lots more Waugh, including the war trilogy and *Brideshead*, how pleasurable it is to examine someone else's bookshelf, you can tell a lot about a person by their book choices, Jesse Russell seemed to have good taste, as far as I could tell, although several of the titles and authors meant nothing to me at all, where sex was concerned Cleo and I had an arrangement, Lady Mary went to bed first, at ten, half an hour later I would perform my ablutions then retire to Jesse's bedroom on the ground floor, when I had finished in the bathroom it was Cleo's turn, Lady Mary retired to bed and read there for twenty minutes, then put out the light and went to sleep, some forty minutes after this, when her mother was asleep, Cleo would tiptoe downstairs in her nightie, barefooted, she would come into my room, slip off her nightie, and we'd fuck, every night, it was a quiet, comfortable sort of fucking, Cleo would lie on her back, I would slip between her thighs and after a few minutes coition would be achieved, Cleo liked to fuck with her eyes closed, savouring every moment I liked to think, the more fool me, anyway, on the occasion of that first visit to Barley House, which lasted five days, Cleo tiptoed downstairs each night, I was a lusty young fellow, once a night was *no problemo*, a satisfying ten-minute squelch, followed by a good night's sleep, what more can a young man hope for? but on the fifth and final night something happened, all went according to plan, Cleo lay naked in her brother's bed, I slipped inside her and began my slow, gentle pumping, I didn't want to come too fast, I always enjoyed taking my time, I liked looking at Cleo's astonishingly beautiful face, at her long black hair, her plump voluptuous breasts, I rose and fell upon her perfect body like a wave on a great ocean, I glanced down at my penis as it slid in and out of Cleo's immense jet-black bush, she was spectacularly hairy, as I penetrated her dense foliage a whiff of salt and weeds tickled my nostrils, and then, suddenly, I became aware that something was, at that precise moment, different, was it a strange noise? was it the subtle play of light and shadow? was it a vague strange elderly scent of mothballs? something had changed, something (as wrinkly ol' Sam Beckett would once remark) happened, I went on pumping but let my gaze slither away from Cleo's gorgeous flesh, my concentration drifted, my eyes scanned the room, they reached the doorway, it was wide open, in the doorway stood Lady Mary, she'd quietly opened it, then stood there, stunned into immobility, she stared down at her naked 18-year-old daughter, she stared at her daughter's boyfriend, Hollis Block, she stared at Hollis's pale smooth buttocks as they rose and fell according to the orthodox rhythms of sexual intercourse, I suppose I expected her to begin shouting, I suppose I expected her to clap her hands to her eyes in disgust, horror, revulsion, she did none of those things, the expression on her face was a kind of gentle sadness, Lady Mary was utterly mute, her eyes were dispassionate and uninvolved, like a scientist in a laboratory observing two toads mating, yes, melancholy, that was it, that was the word, she reminded me in that brief moment of a Madonna – of the agonized face of Our Saviour's mother – a face which shone out of a score of classic Renaissance pictures, even as our gaze met I felt a familiar convulsion begin, I could not help myself, I turned away and back to my labour, my body shuddered as it climaxed, I ejaculated, hard, I groaned and grunted and at length fell forward, dripping with sweat, across Cleo's plump soft warm breasts, whispering endearments, I seemed to have closed my eyes, when I opened them and turned back towards the doorway Lady Mary had gone, the door was closed, I began to wonder if I had imagined this strange episode, had someone slipped lysergic acid into my lunchtime lemonade, surely not, no, You are beautiful, Cleo breathed, she kissed me goodbye, See you in the morning, she whispered, smiling, Good night my love, I replied, You are gorgeous, I love you, the dialogue was as banal as it is in these standard circumstances, in the morning, at breakfast, Lady Mary was her usual brisk self, bringing in plates of toast, passing the marmalade, asking if anyone wanted more coffee, I was strangely reminded of Brenda Wilkins, I wondered if Lady Mary would take me aside and have a quiet word, a discussion of matrimony perhaps, the thought of it chilled me to the bone, I wondered if she would talk to Cleo, not so, evidently, for I never mentioned it to Cleo and Cleo never mentioned it to me, *ergo* she didn't know, even when Cleo went off to pack her bag and we were alone together Lady Mary said nothing, I began to think I must have hallucinated the entire episode, it reminded me in a strange way of a letter I'd just read in the Penguin *Collected Essays, Journalism And Letters of George Orwell*, back in his late twenties, long before he was famous or had even published a book, Eric Blair (as he then was) was stranded in Suffolk, he was back home with his parents, who were angry and hostile that he'd given up a well paid job as a policeman in the service of the glorious British Empire, one day, perhaps to escape the claustrophobic atmosphere in that house on Queen Street, Southwold, he walked to the nearby village of Walberswick, he was in the old ruined church there when at the very edge of his vision a man in brown clothing passed behind him and went through an arch, Blair followed the man out into the churchyard and found it empty, the figure had vanished, there was no plausible explanation other than that the man was a ghost, perhaps that of a medieval monk, but in the final sentence of his account Orwell dismisses this detailed experience as a hallucination, when it was time for us to drive back to Norwich Lady Mary gave me a warm hug and said, *Do* come again soon, Hollis, it's been splendid having you as a visitor, Thank you so much for all the marvellous hospitality, I gushed back, I look forward to seeing you again, we embraced, the church bells rang the hour of ten, Lady Mary stood behind us, waving goodbye as we drove away, a tall, slim elegant woman dressed entirely in black, we visited Barley House once a term, and again during the holidays, I remember it was the following Easter we had a memorable quarrel, we were supposed to be going to see a film in Cheltenham but we'd only gone two or three miles when we had a row, I can't even remember what the film was or what the quarrel was about, I do remember Cleo screaming, I hate you! and me getting out of the car, Fuck off! I shouted back, with a lamentable lack of dialogue originality, existentially I was not in a good position as I was now standing in the road and Cleo was revving the engine, then I saw her push down the black car-lock button, she wound down the window a couple of inches, exclaiming You can bloody well walk back to the house! I asked, Where are you off to? Cheltenham, she shrieked, she drove off in a rage, her last words were once again, I hate you!, I set off back to Barley House, I have always been a fast walker, soon I came to a manicule which pointed towards the village and helpfully informed me it was just 3 miles and 186 words away, in those days there were far fewer cars, I strolled along only rarely disturbed by the noise and fumes of an internal combustion engine, I walked beside twinkling ditches, dragonflies flitted by, blue and orange and purple and red, the sky was blue, it was a warm day, and I congratulated myself on escaping from having to see a film that was more Cleo's kind of thing than mine, I can't even recall what it was, but she liked family comedies, warm uplifting romance, and earnest social commentary dramas, I preferred brooding foreign movies with jazz soundtracks and voiceovers, or fringe Hollywood with extreme violence, Sam Peckinpah remains one of my favourite directors, the high brick wall which surrounded Barley House had a crumbling wooden door set in it at the rear, it was never locked, the village was one without recorded crime – or at least nothing of note since a disgruntled servant had poisoned her master's dog in 1957 – the village still talked of that horror, a much greater offence to humanity than such trifles as the Vietnam War or massacres in apartheid South Africa, I slipped through the door and crossed an area of waste land used for burning rubbish and for compost, I passed an old water pump and walked towards the outbuildings, as I drew close I heard a strange noise, a sort of grunt, or perhaps a whimper of pain, it sounded like an animal, it made me think of a bedraggled cat, or perhaps a dog caught in some wire, the sound was coming from a building which had once been used for storing farm machinery back in the days when Barley House had belonged to a local farmer, the door was open and sunlight shone in on a dusty floor which had wisps of straw scattered across it, as my eyes adjusted to the dark interior I observed a rusty lawnmower, a dining table coated in dust, and behind them a discarded mattress, lying on her back on the mattress was Lady Mary, for a hideous instant I thought she was injured in some way, and dying, her legs were bare and bent, her eyes were closed, and her teeth were bared, then I saw that she had removed her skirt and laid it on the ground nearby, along with her neatly folded blouse and her white bra, her knickers had been pulled down to her ankles, her left hand was squeezing her left breast, wedged into her cleavage was a silver crucifix, with the cross facing down towards her stomach, her other hand burrowed in the grey hair at her crotch, a flow of words dribbled from her taut mouth, with particular repetition of Jesus, when finally she opened her eyes she saw me, we stared at each other in silence for sixty seconds, longer, at last I said, I'm so sorry, you see, I thought I heard an animal in pain, I really had no idea, I do apologise, I turned and fled, she caught up with me just as I reached the back door, she had thrown on her blouse and I could tell she had no bra on beneath, one leg of her tights was laddered, her upper lip was bubbly with sweat, her grip on my arm was surprisingly fierce, she wanted me never to tell Cleo, I won't, Lady Mary, she produced a thin smile, I would not want her to think her mother was... She left the sentence incomplete, I promised I would not say a word, a line from childhood broke the surface, Cross my heart and hope to die, she smiled wanly again, she took hold of my wrist, You see I had a very strong physical relationship with my late husband, I miss that side of marriage terribly, and as a Catholic I could never seek to find what I now lack with another man, it would dishonour Lord Henry, it would make a mockery of everything I believe in, and so you see I... I have to find it in another way, more silence, Do I shock you? Not at all, I said I understand, I said, Besides... There was that time you came to my room in the night and saw... what you saw, if anyone should be embarrassed it is surely me, there was a longer silence between us now, Oh Hollis, she said at last, I believe you *do* understand, Cleo is so fortunate to have found you, you are gentle and kind and I believe have a generous soul, alas, some of her previous boyfriends were not like that, one in particular was quite revolting, but let us not dwell on that, she brightened, Let us have a cup of tea, Actually I'd rather have coffee, if you don't mind, I'm not really much of a tea drinker, Coffee it is, then!, her manner was one of exaggerated ebullience, she hoped to steer us back to a comforting normality, but her smile was still glassy, a little tense and stretched, soon the scarlet kettle was starting its low, shrill whistle on the gas ring, it pierced me like those words of hers, Cleo's previous boyfriends? one in particular? I felt a brief stab of jealous anger, Cleo's history was not something I had given any thought to, somehow I had vaguely imagined there was one at most, God damn it, she was only eighteen years old! we sat at the kitchen table and consumed our hot drinks, Lady Mary changed the subject and asked about the university, soon I was blathering about the architecture, the river, the delightful countryside around it, about Crunchy and his gallops, after our drinks she said she'd better go and freshen up, and I said I thought I'd go to my room and continue reading my book, later, Cleo returned, she'd gone to see the film on her own, I'd hoped that by the time she returned she'd have calmed down, but no such luck, she was still furious with me, she announced that we were leaving early and returning to the east tomorrow, I performed a gesture frequently encountered in prose fiction but only very rarely in life, I shrugged, when my brief physical spasm was over I muttered, Fine by me, she slammed the door and stomped off upstairs to her own room, supper that evening was a brittle affair, with Lady Mary desperately trying to get two moody sullen youngsters to participate in a conversation, in the end she gave up and we dined in silence, And I'm *not* coming to your room tonight, Cleo hissed, and she didn't, in some dark, greasy chamber of my mind I half-hoped Lady Mary might pay me a nocturnal visit instead but by 2am I realised this was a preposterous hope, I still wondered what that earlier visit had signified, she claimed she'd just seen the light on in my room and came to see if I was alright, if I needed anything, was that a fiction, cross Cleo was true to her word and the next morning we departed, we drove all the way in absolute silence, each of us simmering with ill-feeling, the lush, hilly, yellow-stoned Cotswolds faded behind us, by the time we reached the Fens the desolation all around us seemed the perfect correlative of our mood, a vast featureless waste unfolded in every direction, fragmented by ditches which spread out like fissures in a landscape, obstructions and barriers had been carelessly dropped from a great height, we reached our city and Cleo dropped me at the university, while she went off to the house she shared with four other girls, neither of us said a word, there was no kiss, or a see-you-tomorrow, it seemed like the end, two days later... a knock at my door... surprise!.. Cleo standing there, white-faced, yes, I have never forgotten, her cheeks really were the colour of chalk or a nice fresh sheet of printer paper... mutely she held out her hands... language had died in her throat, in her heart, she really couldn't speak, a thudding need had paralysed her... I took hold of her, pressed her against me, I was stupidly weak, stupidly kind, I have always regretted it... makes me think sometimes of that song on *Planet Waves*... I peeled away her clothes, slipped off mine, she lay on her back on the carpet, I plunged in... she brightened... she still loved me, she whispered... she was very, very sorry for being so horrid... that posh girl's vocabulary!... she began to cry... it was good to feel those old magnificent familiar warm breasts crushed against my slim bone-corrugated chest... I said I was sorry too... O, O, O, the insincerity... one-hundred-and-twenty-two seconds later my ejaculations took liquid form... how sweet it is to be connected and carnally cacophonous... Cleo rarely made any noise during sex but on this occasion... she cried out, sobbed and throbbed... she stuck her fierce scarlet woman's fingernails into my pale rear cheeks... later I discovered that I had bled from her ardour... a technique I suspect she'd learned from the movies... Hollywood dictated and dictates so much, so much... a fortnight later we were back at Barley House, Cleo had been invited to a girls' weekend in Cheltenham with some of her old friends from the posh school she'd attended there, Lady Mary drove her there on Saturday morning, having arranged to collect her on Sunday afternoon, the girls were staying at an expensive hotel in the middle of town, it was a no-males weekend and I assured Cleo that I was perfectly happy staying behind at Barley House, I was going through a Charles Dickens phase at the time, working my way through all the fat books, I had managed *David Copperfield*, *Bleak House*, *Little Dorrit* and now I was immersed in *Our Mutual Friend*, what a golden time that was for English scholarship! the biographical introduction to the Penguin English Library edition, written oddly enough by a man, soothingly explained that in 1858 Dickens dumped his wife Catherine ['Kate'] Hogarth and subsequently 'befriended a young actress', although as we now know* it was more a case of begin-fling-with-young-actress-first, *then* dump the wife, *see *The Invisible Woman* by Claire Tomalin, the first detailed account of Dickens's hot relationship with a gal called Nelly, in the revised paperback edition new evidence is published suggesting that Dickens's death was not quite as previously reported, it seems likely that the wrinkled old goat may well have joined the ranks of those fortunate few (Jacob Bronowski, Adam Faith) who expired whilst in the throes of intercourse, like the guy in *Whore*, what a way to go! (smiley face), poor Nelly (solemn caring face), complete exoneration for his behaviour was granted by our Penguin scholar because 'Although Kate, a shadowy, slow person, had given him ten children, she had never suited his exuberant personality very well', yeah, right... anyway, there I was curled up on the sofa with Charles D when Lady Mary's car returned up the drive, I heard the crunching of gravel, the slam of a car door, the quick sharp stab of footsteps, her shadow flashed across the leaded bay window, I had just reached page 180 and Mr Podsnap's disquisition on the English male, *There is in the Englishman a combination of qualities, a modesty, an independence, a responsibility, a repose, combined with an absence of everything calculated to call a blush into the cheek of a young person, which one would seek in vain among the Nations of the Earth*, Cup of tea?, Lady Mary enquired, she stood in the doorway, tall, slim, elegant, dressed in a black trouser outfit with a trimmed fur collar, a faint perfumed fragrance drifted into the room, I declined, she seemed to have forgotten my disdain for that bourgeois restorative, she smiled, Perhaps something stronger? Such as? Whisky? A gin and tonic? I glanced at the ticking clock in the corner, it was a few minutes before 11am, the time when pubs across the land opened, her smile deepened, as did the wrinkles around her eyes, I'll join you if you say yes, I said Yes, when she returned from the kitchen she was carrying a surprisingly large tumbler of malt for me and a gin and tonic for herself, she settled beside me on the sofa, I took a first few sips of the whisky and felt it burn through my blood, it was far too early in the day to be knocking back spirits, she rested her hand on my knee, Not to beat about the bush, Hollis, she said quietly, Would you make love to me? If that isn't an entirely repellent prospect... I gulped down what was left in my tumbler, a steel band began making a hollow booming racket inside me, she smiled, This is a purely physical proposition, you understand, I am not trying to steal you away from my daughter, or any nonsense like that, unable to speak, I nodded, I am not in love with you, obviously, the very idea would be absurd, but what *is* absurd is that I have this very powerful need for physical affection and no one to satisfy it, at least, no one I have ever wanted to satisfy it, she finished her drink, began another, and continued, I have had offers, you understand, various men in the village, as well as friends of my husband, some men think that the first thing a widow needs after her bereavement is a fresh penis in her life, forgive me for speaking frankly, but everyone who has ever offered that kind of consolation was repugnant to me, the very idea was disgusting to me, and as you know, although I *did* and *do* have physical needs I was able to satisfy them in my own way – but then you entered my life, I think I knew quite quickly that you are a good, kind person – someone who has finer feelings than the average male – and what is more you are insanely attractive, she laid her other hand upon me, Ah,

Hollis, I see that your flesh is willing – but is the spirit? believe me I will not hold it against you if you choose not to hold it against me – or to put it another way, if you reject my suggestion, she chuckled, an unexpected spasm on her part, her elegant cheeks were now flushed from all that gin, Catholics can be surprisingly heavy drinkers, I realise, she continued, pouring herself another, I must seem quite disgustingly old, but I like to think I am in reasonable shape for a woman of my age... Er, yes, Hollis said, his voice was a nervous croak, Actually I find you very attractive indeed, this is beginning to sound like *The Graduate,* n'est-ce-pas? Then let us to bed, her ebullience seemed a little forced, it was probably nerves, she took his hand and led Hollis upstairs, but instead of going to her own bedroom she took him to one of the guest rooms, inside it was immense, with a four-poster bed and a fireplace, this was Eleanor and Ambrose's room, it smelled of perfume, evidently Eleanor adored dowsing herself in fragrance, on the dressing table were many small square and oval bottles bearing names of which only one – Chanel – I recognised, she explained, I cannot engage in the physical in my own room, you understand, it would seem sacrilegious, it would insult the memory of my long and happy marriage to Henry, I nodded, it was fine by me where we went, I had no particular preference, Do take your clothes off, Hollis, and get into bed, I will join you shortly, H did as she requested, although with a slight feeling of nervousness, he was sure he'd read a short story about a man who climbed into bed, only to find that instead of his naked lover the next person to enter the room was a man with a cosh, but then Hollis remembered that that had been a story about an adulterous love affair, the man with the cosh was the angry husband, he need have no such worries, because Lord Henry Russell was dead, his widow returned shortly, she was now wearing a light cotton gown, which she slipped off, I saw that she'd removed her outer garments but kept on her stockings and suspender belt, she was right, she was in remarkable shape for a woman whose hair was silvery-white, both around her head and in the trim, velvety bush where her body forked, she tore back the sheet and joined me in that immense bed, I had never been in a four-poster bed before, Lady Mary leaned over me, she sniffed me as if my hair held a fine perfume, the long slender fingers of her right hand brushed against my expectation, Oh God, she said, Forgive me, then she lay back and whispered, Come inside me, Hollis, to my surprise she was dripping with sexual juices – far more so than her daughter ever was, Cleo I had always found a little on the dry side, and I frequently had to use saliva as a lubricant, we began the old ceremony, Lady Mary began to whisper that she was a sinner, that the Lord must forgive her, I knew at once she wasn't talking to me, like Julian of Norwich she was having a one-to-one with her saviour, she spoke of depravity, of great wickedness, of betrayal of trust, I felt that a part of her was excited by her speech, was aroused by it, enjoyed it, used it as an engine to speed her on the pathway to her bliss, she soon reached it, as did Hollis, his seed emptying into her barren womb, in the distance I heard the village church strike noon, I want you to make love to me again later, Lady Mary said, But first I think we should have some luncheon, a splendid idea! despite everything which had happened I still felt somewhat in awe of Lady Mary, she was the quintessence of exquisite refinement, dressed once again – for one never knew when Father Grassam might make one of his surprise visits – she exuded elegance, she had a remarkable face, with a firm jaw, high cheek bones, an aquiline nose, a pale, clear complexion and a rich head of hair which billowed down to her shoulders, she belonged in an elegant Jamesian novel of the lives of the affluent, not in some tawdry postmodern tale written without paragraph breaks, around her neck hung that impressive crucifix, she was like her daughter but taller, thinner, with smaller breasts, and hair which had aged, as everyone's does in time, Cleo in fact was quite a big girl, with big child-bearing thighs, handsome breasts, the haunches of a horse, we sat at the immense scratched wooden table in the kitchen and dined on half a dozen fine cheeses, tomatoes, a brown loaf from the village baker, apple juice produced by a local farmer, and a delicious ham, also local, for dessert there was a carrot cake, also from the local bakery, a feast, our conversation refrained from the vulgar topic of our recent carnal activity, instead we discussed literature, I blathered about Charles Dickens, Lady Mary told me I should read Cardinal Newman, we found common ground with Gerard Manley Hopkins, we both agreed he was terrific, I'd had to do him for 'A Level', his visionary intensity had excited me, his language was sensual and intense, *The world is charged with the grandeur of God. / It will shine out like shining from shook foil*, you didn't have to be a Jesuit to feel the electricity, in fact Gerard Manley Hopkins has always reminded me of Van Gogh, feel the power coursing through those shimmering fields and in the throbbing sky, yes, after coffee she took my hand again, I want to make love under the sky, she said, Hollis let her lead him to the rear of the house, they came to a sunlit glade in the apple orchard, wasps buzzed around our heads, they removed their clothes and stood facing each other like Adam and Eve, his semi-erect penis pointed at her like a direction sign: *Orgasm – 200 yards*, she touched it gingerly with her fingers, then wetly, kneeling, with her mouth, her attentions made it rise up before her like a gorgeous mushroom with a tall stem and a narrow cap, it was the kind of moment which required a Nabokov to capture and express it – a style which would combine the saliva-glisten of lewd pornography with a literary elegance that matched the bone-structure of the elderly lustful face that had folded itself over Hollis's most precious possession, he cupped his hands around Lady Mary's head and stared down at her silky ash-pale hair, he released a groan that seemed to match the volume of the distant church bell tolling a single resonant chime, she looked up at him like a weary triumphant vampire, a dribble fell from the corners of her mouth, down her chin, to drop and join the few remaining drops of dew which dappled that honest English grass, she lay down on the grass, still a little damp despite all that sunshine, and Hollis repaid the compliment until she pushed him away and instructed him to come inside, to his astonishment she starts talking dirty, she whispers to the Lord, making her confession, her voice deepening, speeding up, she says she's a slut, a dirty whore, a filthy whore who has carnal knowledge of her daughter's boyfriend, she says she deserves to be taken, on the compost heap, amid the rotting fruit and the worms, she is worthless, she should be smeared in mud, in muck, in filth, but this is all fantasy, it is what she excites her, she, the devout Catholic, filth and sin excite, they heighten pleasure, that tormenting physical craving, the bittersweet sugar and vinegar, the agony, that evening Lady Mary cooks us dinner but she has barely started in the kitchen when the telephone rings, it is Cleo, she asks to speak to me, she wants to know what I have been up to in her absence, nothing, much, as a Tudor wit might write, and you? she and the other girls went out for afternoon tea, they talked, she and her gossips gossiped, tonight they are off out for a meal, their hotel is OK but there was a broken glass in her bathroom and one of the towels wasn't clean, I sympathise, standards aren't what they used to be, I miss you my love, she says, And you, I reply, she asks to speak to mummy, she confirms the time and place for her to be collected, outside The Pump Room – the Pump Room! - at two tomorrow, mummy, Yes, darling, I'll be there, rump steak, Lady Mary buys it for Cleo's brother (always absent, Hollis never meets him during the course of this tawdry improbable raggedy tale), she keeps it in the freezer, big 'n' juicy, oh yes, yes, a candlelit supper for two, candles, a tall stem of wax which burns at the tip, oh yes, yes, sizzle of fat, bubble of seething flesh, onions scorched along the edge, rich dark mushrooms with soft curling lips, exquisite meat, that Tudor wit again, and afterwards profiteroles, a layer of dark chocolate and pastry masking a creamy delicious ball of cream, ball of cream, having a ball, yes ma'am, the church bell tolls, oh more, more, let us roll all our strength and all our sweetness up into one ball and tear our pleasures with rough strife through the iron gates of life, all washed down with one of the brother's bottled beers and several glasses of a rather fine Portuguese red, I trace back a lifetime's appreciation – hic! – of the varying textures and flavours of the grape to that unforgettable evening, the wine that night was smooth, velvety, as exquisite as a lover's body, as silky as the blurb for an acclaimed new novel in *The Bookseller*, later we retired to the bedroom of scented Eleanor and odious Ambrose, soon we were making whoopee – or starting to – her tongue lingered on my precious sceptre, my fingers burrowed in her shrubbery, but then she took hold of my wrist and detached my digits from her sultry pit, I want you to do something, she said, she looked apprehensive, as if I might say no, or be angry, she whispered in my ear, my pulse accelerated, I recalled the splendid motto of my university, Very well, I said, I'll give it a go, she handed me a small pot of Nivea, This might make it easier, she whispered, shy as a fifteen-year-old on her first fuck, Lady Mary rocked and rolled, she scrutinised her pillow, she presented her asset, the tulip-shaped tip of my gift bumped against walls of bone and sheets of muscular skin, it scraped against her grey, velvety pubic hair, I was reminded of the time years later when after a long walk across moorland and through a scented pine forest I went in search of the entrance to Koreez Cave, which was located amid undergrowth on the side of a very steep hill above a lake in a land hollowed by glaciers, up a bit, down a bit, you'll get there in the end, it is easy to become disappointed, to let ambition wilt, to give up and melt back into a conventional mode, then inspiration came, I deleted all thoughts of ziggurats and walkways on stilts and thought instead of my old school's motto, weighted with classical value, *Paulatim ergo certe*, it did the trick, I performed my labour, I felt myself suddenly in a new-found-land, a dark landscape which was emptier, somehow more spacious, with an occasional rubbery sensation, as if sea sponges drifted gently there, propelled by a slow, gentle muddy current, Lady Mary began to squirm, to articulate her sweet self-disgust, we were back to filth and sin, to a human worm, a wretch beyond all forgiveness, her confession was littered with astonishing obscenities, the depth – the dark hot maggoty depths – of a Catholic can truly amaze, she had gone much further into language than sweating tormented drenched-in-radiance masturbating Gerard Manley Hopkins, for she was finally there with Saint Julian, wet with Jesuitical ecstasy, loud with the actual Lord's incandescent high-voltage connection, a Wordsworthian cataract, foaming, creamy, thunderous, terrific, shuddering her into dreams of herring and blood and knives and nails, I had to seize hold of her convulsing pelvis, I had to haul her back from paradise otherwise she'd have been wrenched away from that rope-thick thread which joined us, our mutual convulsions and moanings and gasps brought this acute, intense narrative episode to a conventional conclusion, we were soaked in sweat, flushed, limp with achievement, barely able to breathe, my stomach pressed against the tiny ridges of her long spine, a good seven or eight minutes may have passed before either of us spoke, then, finally, she said in a rich accent lined with velvet and weighted with sweet rich juicy plums, and I said, and it was not for many years that I learned that the date on which this event occurred was the anniversary of Lord Henry's death, which may or may not explain her motive... H woke at seven... on his side.. pressed against Lady Mary's warm back... the bedding had slipped off in the night... lay there like nude survivors of a shipwreck, adrift on a raft... naturally H had an erection – H always did when he woke – he felt a pleasant thrill of anticipation... his precious sceptre was snugly framed by the adjacent twin mounds, it was like a missile ready to be fired, the name *Peenemünde* came to mind, Hollis was still half-asleep, he remembered he had been dreaming, in his dream a shot had been fired, he was on an ocean liner and it was night and someone was in the shadows by the nearest lifeboats, whoever this person was they were armed, the shot missed but catapulted him from the flimsy fabric of this drama back into the Cotswolds and Eleanor's bedroom at Barley House, as he lay there he heard movement downstairs, there was the distinct sound of footsteps moving around the house, this is as good as a movie, a TV drama, exquisitely English, lovely furniture, beautiful house in the countryside, a ticking clock, a barometer, a storm is on its way, the symbols are laid out on the marble mantelpiece, the rippling willows outside ripple with unease, sub-philharmonic music begins playing, the pace speeds up, the village pub with its shining brasses and merry landlord are allowed a brief glimpse, this is the quintessence of Englishness, rural, tranquil, yet steeped in filth, packed with secrets, for some reason hearing those steps below I thought it must be Ambrose Roar arriving, he had a habit of arriving unannounced, it wasn't, it was not him at all, a moment later the bedroom door creaked open, a surge of muted light spilled from a corridor, a hand reached for the light switch, the room filled with brightness, a moment of terrible clarity and then the sudden tightening of face muscles, the contortion of a mouth, the howl of human anguish, *Mummy, how could you!* Cleo of course, why must life imitate cliché, the dreariest of plot devices, the lustful transgressors surprised in bed, Cleo's beautiful, elegant face muscles ran through a stark and dismal repertoire of actressy emotions – incredulity, shock, anger, misery, disbelief, belief, misery again, and again anger, which blazed up into fury – I can't believe I wrote that, I'll leave it in though it ought to be deleted, by now Lady Mary was awake, her face turned a considerably whiter shade of pale, deathly white probably, I won't know until I've seen a corpse, she heaved herself off the bed, those very slightly wrinkled dugs, that magnificent marble rear, the splendid silvery hair, there was a whiff, several whiffs, a complex alchemy, lust, terror, horror, perhaps even the faintest hint of faeces, her body shook, how it shook! – spasms of guilt, of – again – horror, she walked towards her daughter and reached out her arms, as if to embrace her, *Don't fucking touch me!* Cleo screeched, Lady Mary nodded, I am so, so sorry, my darling, this tale calls out for a screenplay, a hotshot agent, a lucrative deal, I could get a better car, possibly an infinity pool, As for you! – Cleo had swivelled to face me – swivelling is an excellent behavioural skill for difficult situations – Get out of this fucking house you pathetic piece of shit! or so I imagine she said, I really can't remember after all this time, You mustn't blame Hollis, Lady Mary said, I am the one to blame, it is all my fault, absolutely, totally, one-hundred percent, probably she didn't say that at all, but that was the gist, an articulation of Catholic guilt, although you might wonder if she didn't experience a certain quiet satisfaction as she later narrated it inside a Catholic telephone box to the goggle-eyed red-cheeked elderly virgin with skin like an old wrinkled peach the other side of the wizard's curtain, all I recall is that she was magnificent in her calm suffering dignity, but Cleo would not be placated, why should she, she was full of rage and bitterness, her eyes bulged with venom, if such a thing is possible, it may not be, she had swivelled again, Get the fuck out! I never want to see you again, ever! these commands addressed to yours truly, I exited the bed, impressively you might think my organ of desire was still almost vertical, although under this new verbal onslaught it had started to sway and was on the brink of wilting, for a wild crazy moment I thought maybe we could work something out, invite Cleo to join us, we could have a peacekeeping threesome and negotiate an amiable, amicable, agreeable carnal arrangement for the years that lay ahead of us, in retrospect that still seems to me to have been an admirable idea, I should have been a diplomat, sadly Cleo was in no mood for compromise or reconciliation, her language became coarser, more heated, more deplorable, Okay, okay! I said, I performed the narrative gestures expected of a character at such moments, I shrugged, I raised my hands in mock surrender, I'm going!, my wanton expectations had quite collapsed, my miserable worm was nestled on its bed of plums, the plumstones seemed big and hard, I'm sure I ached, I felt exhausted, I slipped on my Marks and Spencer underpants, my blue jeans, my grey socks and scarlet T-shirt, on the way out of the room I solemnly shook hands with Lady Mary, who just stood there, naked, elegant, looking dazed and distraught, she was in shock, I suppose, and then of course there was the weight of all that Catholic guilt, it was as if the Cumberland Stone had been placed on her back, I left mother and daughter to sort out their domestic differences among themselves and went downstairs to the absent male sibling's room, where I packed my things, heaved my rucksack on to my back, and quietly left the house to walk to the bus stop by the village pub, at this time of day there were several buses to Cheltenham and from there I could catch a train back to Norwich, that is what I did, I took a last look at Barley House and its willow trees and then I walked away from place forever, I have never been back, I did not know it then but I was walking towards Militká, she was out there, she would have been 46 that year, we never know what we roll and rock towards in time, a banal truism but all the same true, and long after Militká, years and years later, in the twenty-first century, Lady Mary died at the age of one-hundred-and-one, I happened to see the obituary in *The Times*, it paid tribute to her work for charity and the deep importance of her faith, she never remarried and she remained at Barley House until almost the end, perhaps once or twice she thought of me, I'll never know, it's November now, a cold wind is blowing outside, rain comes and goes in soft autumnal showers, I did not see Cleo again for three months, when she finally came to my door and announced that she had forgiven me, she recognised she said that what had occurred was not primarily my fault, could we get back together? I nodded, and we peeled off our clothes and got into bed, later I asked her why she'd turned up at Barley House that morning when she was supposed to be in Cheltenham until 4pm, the explanation was Agatha-Christie-simple, her hotel had caught fire, obliging all the guests to depart in the middle of the night, the other girls had all wanted to go home early too, taxis had been shared to get them to their destinations, we did not talk about her mother, Cleo said that after all we'd been through she felt she could now say things she'd never said before, the first revelation was that she'd never had an orgasm with me or any other lover, she'd been faking, secondly, she wanted me to do something which she thought would help, I said I would be happy to, and then she told me what it was, lawks a mercy! these Catholic backgrounds... what would the Pope think?... humiliated by her first confession − he had no heart − no heart to deny her − peculiar though her request was − she wanted him to − to do it − yes, while dressed in her clothes − duly obliged − a good sport − dragged on her stockings − she assisted with her bra − filled the generous cups with a pair of Guadeloupe melons − applied to him her brightest shade of red did she − would have liked him to wear a pair of her high-heeled shoes − but size eleven feet were just too big − set to work − did she come? − said yes, yes, oh yes... − H not totally convinced − the relationship dragged on for another year... but... they kept quarrelling and in the end it fizzled out... there was no grand rupture... simply a gradual drifting apart... besides... a dark, Lady-Mary-shaped shadow... lay between... could never be dissolved... Cleo and H went to bed less and less... when she moved to the coast H did not follow her... stayed behind... would never wear lipstick or stockings or a bra again... as lovers do, lost touch... not for many years did H discover... Cleo had re-invented herself as a lesbian... perhaps −

thinking about that strange underwear request – perhaps she always was one... the internet arrived... from time to time H looked her up... Cleo tweets, furiously... up to speed on current issues... gay rights... sexual identity... holds progressive views on transgender issues... solemnly registers with RIP the deaths of famous singers... intermittently gutted... writers... film stars... plus posts pics... cute kitten, hilarious pug puppy... emotes about... badly treated animals... does not disguise her feelings about unpopular politicians... ghastly Farage, Trump, blustering BoJo... boxes ticked... also on Facebook... there I learned of her years in Thailand, her brother's wedding in Melbourne, her trip to Antarctica... she adores Jeanette Winterson and Sarah Waters... loved *Blue is the Warmest Colour* and *La-la Land* and both the Paddington Bear movies... for some years she had a cat named Fred... today Cleo lives in Lisbon with her lover... a rather beautiful young Portuguese woman... their last holiday was in Rio... Cleo appears happy... I am happy too, happy she's found contentment... none of her online posts has ever mentioned *moi*... or my scribblings... that's how I like it... it's only rock'n'roll... dispersal point time... oh yes... the caaaaarnival is over... send in the clowns... the afternoons grow dark... winter is almost here... the coastal road is repeatedly flooded... I'm not *that* hard to track down, if you seriously want to... Pat did... so did Natasha from Moscow... a man cannot change his surname as easily as a woman... Cleo plainly has no interest... she is utterly indifferent... so be it... sad face... another bright day dawns, exclamation mark... a cup of tea in bed before the descent... a page or two of the Frenchman... Phil's favourite singer was Linda Ronstadt... Phil liked the easy-listening station... put the book down... glance on my phone at the obituary of another favourite writer, also a Frenchman, at the end *This obituary has been revised and updated since the obituary writer's own death...* now time to shave, shower, dress... a few gobbles of Diazepam... ye canna beat a fistful o'

drugs to make the day seem brighter, cheerier... smiley face!...
now down to breakfast... so-so coffee... the silver rack... the
poached egg solid inside... Excuse me! hello! I say, there... could
I have more toast, please?